THE PRESENCE OF GRACE

BOOKS BY J. F. POWERS

The Presence of Grace

Prince of Darkness

THE
PRESENCE
OF
GRACE

J. F. POWERS

1956

DOUBLEDAY & COMPANY, INC.

GARDEN CITY, NEW YORK

*All of the characters in this book are fictitious,
and any resemblance to actual persons,
living or dead, is purely coincidental.*

Library of Congress Catalog Card Number 56–5963

"*Dawn,*" *from* Partisan Review. *Copyright 1956 by Partisan Review.*
"*Death of a Favorite,*" *from* The New Yorker. *Copyright 1950 by The
New Yorker Magazine, Inc.*
"*The Poor Thing,*" *from* Tomorrow. *Copyright 1949 by Garrett Pub-
lications.*
"*The Devil Was the Joker,*" *from* The New Yorker. *Copyright 1953
by The New Yorker Magazine, Inc.*
"*A Losing Game,*" *from* The New Yorker. *Copyright 1955 by The
New Yorker Magazine, Inc.*
"*Defection of a Favorite,*" *from* The New Yorker. *Copyright 1951 by
The New Yorker Magazine, Inc.*
"*Zeal,*" *from* Commonweal.
"*Blue Island,*" *from* Accent. *Copyright 1955 by Accent.*
"*The Presence of Grace,*" *from* Accent. *Copyright 1954 by Accent.*

TO BETTY

CONTENTS

THE PRESENCE OF GRACE

CHAPTER II

THE PRINCE OF PEACE

DAWN

Father Udovic placed the envelope before the Bishop and stepped back. He gave the Bishop more than enough time to read what was written on the envelope, time to digest *The Pope* and, down in the corner, the *Personal,* and then he stepped forward. "It was in the collection yesterday," he said. "At Cathedral."

"Peter's Pence, Father?"

Father Udovic nodded. He'd checked that. It had been in with the special Peter's Pence envelopes, and not with the regular Sunday ones.

"Well, then . . ." The Bishop's right hand opened over the envelope, then stopped, and came to roost again, uneasily, on the edge of the desk.

Father Udovic shifted a foot, popped a knuckle in his big toe. The envelope was a bad thing all right. They'd never received anything like it. The Bishop was doing what Father Udovic had done when confronted by the envelope, thinking twice, which was what Monsignor Renton at Cathedral had done, and his curates before him, and his housekeeper who counted the collection. In the end, each had seen the envelope as a hot potato and passed it on. But the Bishop

11

couldn't do that. He didn't know *what* might be inside. Even Father Udovic, who had held it up to a strong light, didn't know. That was the hell of it.

The Bishop continued to stare at the envelope. He still hadn't touched it.

"It beats me," said Father Udovic, moving backwards. He sank down on the leather sofa.

"Was there something else, Father?"

Father Udovic got up quickly and went out of the office—wondering how the Bishop would handle the problem, disappointed that he evidently meant to handle it by himself. In a way, Father Udovic felt responsible. It had been his idea to popularize the age-old collection—"to personalize Peter's Pence"—by moving the day for it ahead a month so that the Bishop, who was going to Rome, would be able to present the proceeds to the Holy Father personally. There had been opposition from the very first. Monsignor Renton, the rector at Cathedral, and one of those at table when Father Udovic proposed his plan, was ill-disposed to it (as he was to Father Udovic himself) and had almost killed it with his comment, "Smart promotion, Bruno." (Monsignor Renton's superior attitude was understandable. He'd had Father Udovic's job, that of chancellor of the diocese, years ago, under an earlier bishop.) But Father Udovic had won out. The Bishop had written a letter incorporating Father Udovic's idea. The plan had been poorly received in some rectories, which was to be expected since it disturbed the routine schedule of special collections. Father Udovic, however, had been confident that the people, properly appealed to, could do better than in the past with Peter's Pence. And the first returns, which had reached him that afternoon, were reassuring—whatever the envelope might be.

It was still on the Bishop's desk the next day, off to one side, and it was there on the day after. On the following day, Thursday, it was in the "In" section of his file basket. On Friday it was still there, buried. Obviously the Bishop was stumped.

On Saturday morning, however, it was back on the desk. Father Udovic, called in for consultation, had a feeling, a really satisfying feeling, that the Bishop might have need of him. If so, he would be ready. He had a plan. He sat down on the sofa.

"It's about this," the Bishop said, glancing down at the envelope before him. "I wonder if you can locate the sender."

"I'll do my best," said Father Udovic. He paused to consider whether it would be better just to go and do his best, or to present his plan of operation to the Bishop for approval. But the Bishop, not turning to him at all, was outlining what he wanted done. And it was Father Udovic's own plan! The Cathedral priests at their Sunday Masses should request the sender of the envelope to report to the sacristy afterwards. The sender should be assured that the contents would be turned over to the Holy Father, if possible.

"Providing, of course," said Father Udovic, standing and trying to get into the act, "it's not something . . ."

"Providing it's possible to do so."

Father Udovic tried not to look sad. The Bishop might express himself better, but he was saying nothing that hadn't occurred to Father Udovic first, days before. It was pretty discouraging.

He retreated to the outer office and went to work on a memo of their conversation. Drafting letters and announcements was the hardest part of his job for him. He tended to go astray without a memo, to take up with the tempting clichés that came to him in the act of composition and sometimes perverted the Bishop's true meaning. Later that morning he called Monsignor Renton and read him the product of many revisions, the two sentences.

"Okay," said Monsignor Renton. "I'll stick it in the bulletin. Thanks a lot."

As soon as Father Udovic hung up, he doubted that that was what the Bishop wished. He consulted the memo. The Bishop was very anxious that "not too much be made of this matter." Naturally, Monsignor Renton wanted the item for his parish bulletin. He was hard up. At one time he had produced the best bulletin in the diocese, but now he was written out, quoting more and more from the magazines and even from the papal encyclicals. Father Udovic called Monsignor Renton back and asked that the announcement be kept out of print. It would be enough to read it once over lightly from the pulpit, using Father Udovic's version because it said enough without saying too much and was, he implied, authorized by the Bishop. Whoever the announcement concerned would comprehend it. If published, the announcement would be subject to study and private interpretation. "Announcements from the pulpit are soon forgotten," Father Udovic said. "I mean—by the people they don't concern."

"You were right the first time, Bruno," said Monsignor Renton. He sounded sore.

The next day—Sunday—Father Udovic stayed home, expecting a call from Monsignor Renton, or possibly even a visit. There was nothing. That evening he called the Cathedral rectory and got one of the curates. Monsignor Renton wasn't expected in until very late. The curate had made the announcement at his two Masses, but no one had come to him about it. "Yes, Father, as you say, it's quite possible someone came to Monsignor about it. Probably he didn't consider it important enough to call you about."

"*Not important!*"

"Not important enough to call *you* about, Father. On *Sunday*."

"I see," said Father Udovic mildly. It was good to know that the curate, after almost a year of listening to Monsignor Renton, was still respectful. Some of the men out in parishes said Father Udovic's job was a snap and maintained that he'd landed it only because he employed the touch system of typing. Before hanging up, Father Udovic stressed the importance of resolving the question of the envelope, but somehow (words played tricks on him) he sounded as though he were accusing the curate of indifference. What a change! The curate didn't take criticism very well, as became all too clear from his sullen silence, and he wasn't very loyal. When Father Udovic suggested that Monsignor Renton might have neglected to make the announcement at his Masses, the curate readily agreed. "Could've slipped his mind all right. I guess you know what that's like."

Early the next morning Father Udovic was in touch with Monsignor Renton, beginning significantly with a glowing report on the Peter's Pence collection, but the conversation languished, and finally he had to ask about the announcement.

"Nobody showed," Monsignor Renton said in an annoyed voice. "What d'ya want to do about it?"

"Nothing right now," said Father Udovic, and hung up. If there had been a failure in the line of communication, he thought he knew where it was.

The envelope had reposed on the Bishop's desk over the weekend and through most of Monday. But that afternoon Father Udovic, on one of his appearances in the Bishop's office, noticed that it was gone. As soon as the Bishop left for the day, Father Udovic rushed in, looking first in the wastebasket, then among the sealed outgoing letters, for a moment actually expecting to see a fat one addressed in the Bishop's hand to the Apostolic Delegate. When he uncovered the envelope in the "Out" section of the file basket, he wondered at himself for looking in the other places first. The envelope had to be filed somewhere—a separate folder would be best—but Father Udovic didn't file it. He carried it to his desk. There, sitting down to it in the gloom of the outer office, weighing, feeling, smelling the envelope, he succumbed entirely to his first fears. He remembered the parable of the cockle. "An enemy hath done this." An enemy was plotting to disturb the peace of the diocese, to employ the Bishop as an agent against himself, or against some other innocent person, some unsuspecting priest or nun—yes, against Father Udovic. Why him? Why not? Only a diseased mind would contemplate such a scheme, Father Udovic thought, but that didn't make it less likely. And the sender, whoever he was, doubtless anonymous and judging others by himself, would assume that the envelope had already been opened and that the announcement was calculated to catch him. Such a person would never come forward.

Father Udovic's fingers tightened on the envelope. He could rip it open, but he wouldn't. That evening, enjoying instant coffee in his room, he could steam it open. But he wouldn't. In the beginning, the envelope might have been opened. It would have been so easy, pardonable then. Monsignor Renton's housekeeper might have done it. With the Bishop honoring the name on the envelope and the intentions of whoever wrote it, up to a point anyway, there was now a principle operating that just couldn't be bucked. Monsignor Renton could have it his way.

That evening Father Udovic called him and asked that the announcement appear in the bulletin.

"Okay. I'll stick it in. It wouldn't surprise me if we got some action now."

"I hope so," said Father Udovic, utterly convinced that Monsignor Renton had failed him before. "Do you mind taking it down verbatim this time?"

"Not at all."

In the next bulletin, an advance copy of which came to Father Udovic through the courtesy of Monsignor Renton, the announcement appeared in an expanded, unauthorized version.

The result on Sunday was no different.

During the following week, Father Udovic considered the possibility that the sender was a floater and thought of having the announcement broadcast from every pulpit in the diocese. He would need the Bishop's permission for that, though, and he didn't dare to ask for something he probably wouldn't get. The Bishop had instructed him not to make too much of the matter. The sender would have to be found at Cathedral, or not at all. If not at all, Father Udovic, having done his best, would understand that he wasn't supposed to know any more about the envelope than he did. He would file it away, and some other chancellor, some other bishop, perhaps, would inherit it. The envelope was most likely harmless anyway, but Father Udovic wasn't so much relieved as bored by the probability that some poor soul was trusting the Bishop to put the envelope into the hands of the Holy Father, hoping for rosary beads blessed by him, or for his autographed picture, and enclosing a small offering, perhaps a spiritual bouquet. Toward the end of the week, Father Udovic told the Bishop that he liked to think that the envelope contained a spiritual bouquet

17

from a little child, and that its contents had already been delivered, so to speak, its prayers and communions already credited to the Holy Father's account in heaven.

"I must say I hadn't thought of that," said the Bishop.

Unfortunately for his peace of mind Father Udovic wasn't always able to believe that the sender was a little child.

The most persistent of those coming to him in reverie was a middle-aged woman saying she hadn't received a special Peter's Pence envelope, had been out of town a few weeks, and so hadn't heard or read the announcement. When Father Udovic tried her on the meaning of the *Personal* on the envelope, however, the woman just went away, and so did all the other suspects under questioning—except one. This was a rich old man suffering from scrupulosity. He wanted his alms to be in secret, as it said in Scripture, lest he be deprived of his eternal reward, but not *entirely* in secret. That was as far as Father Udovic could figure the old man. Who was he? An audacious old Protestant who hated communism, or could some future Knight of St. Gregory be taking his first awkward step? The old man was pretty hard to believe in, and the handwriting on the envelope sometimes struck Father Udovic as that of a woman. This wasn't necessarily bad. Women controlled the nation's wealth. He'd seen the figures on it. The explanation was simple: widows. Perhaps they hadn't taken the right tone in the announcement. Father Udovic's version had been safe and cold, Monsignor Renton's like a summons. It might have been emphasized that the Bishop, under certain circumstances, would *gladly* undertake to deliver the envelope. That might have made a difference. The sender would not only have to appreciate the difficulty of the Bishop's position, but abandon his own. That wouldn't be easy for the sort of person Father Udovic had in mind. He had a feeling that it wasn't going to happen. The Bishop would leave for Rome on the following Tuesday. So time was running out. The envelope could contain a check—quite the cruelest thought—on which payment would be stopped after a limited time by the donor, whom Father Udovic persistently saw as an old person not to be dictated to, or it could be nullified even sooner by untimely death. God, what a shame! In Rome, where the needs of the world, temporal as well as spiritual, were so well known, the Bishop would've been welcome as the flowers in May.

And then, having come full circle, Father Udovic would be hard on himself for dreaming and see the envelope as a whited sepulcher concealing all manner of filth, spelled out in letters snipped from newsprint and calculated to shake Rome's faith in him. It was then that he particularly liked to think of the sender as a little child. But soon the middle-aged woman would be back, and all the others, among whom the hottest suspect was a feeble-minded nun—devils all to pester him, and the last was always worse than the first. For he always ended up with the old man—and what if there was such an old man?

On Saturday, Father Udovic called Monsignor Renton and asked him to run the announcement again. It was all they could do, he said, and admitted that he had little hope of success.

"Don't let it throw you, Bruno. It's always darkest before dawn."

Father Udovic said he no longer cared. He said he liked to think that the envelope contained a spiritual bouquet from a little child, that its contents had already been delivered, its prayers and communions already . . .

"You should've been a nun, Bruno."

"Not sure I know what you mean," Father Udovic said, and hung up. He wished it were in his power to do something about Monsignor Renton. Some of the old ones got funny when they stayed too long in one place.

On Sunday, after the eight o'clock Mass, Father Udovic received a call from Monsignor Renton. "I told 'em if somebody didn't own up to the envelope, we'd open it. I guess I got carried away." But it had worked. Monsignor Renton had just talked with the party responsible for the envelope—a Mrs. Anton—and she was on the way over to see Father Udovic.

"A woman, huh?"

"A widow. That's about all I know about her."

"A widow, huh? Did she say what was in it?"

"I'm afraid it's not what you thought, Bruno. It's money."

Father Udovic returned to the front parlor, where he had left Mrs. Anton. "The Bishop'll see you," he said, and sat down. She wasn't making a good impression on him. She could've used a shave. When she'd asked for the Bishop, Father Udovic had replied instinctively, "He's busy," but it hadn't convinced her. She had appeared quite capable of walking out on him. He invoked the Bishop's name again. "Now one of the things the Bishop'll want to know is why you didn't show up before this."

Mrs. Anton gazed at him, then past him, as she had when he'd tried to question her. He saw her starting to get up, and thought he was about to lose her. He hadn't heard the Bishop enter the room.

The Bishop waved Mrs. Anton down, seated himself near the doorway at some distance from them, and motioned to Father Udovic to continue.

To the Bishop it might sound like browbeating, but Father Udovic meant to go on being firm with Mrs. Anton. He hadn't forgotten that she'd responded to Monsignor Renton's threats. "Why'd you wait so long? You listen to the Sunday announcements, don't you?" If she persisted in ignoring him, she could make him look bad, of course, but he didn't look for her to do that, with the Bishop present.

Calmly Mrs. Anton spoke, but not to Father Udovic. "Call off your trip?"

The Bishop shook his head.

In Father Udovic's opinion, it was one of his functions to protect the Bishop from directness of that sort. "How do we know what's in here?" he demanded. Here, unfortunately, he reached up the wrong sleeve of his cassock for the envelope. Then he had it. "What's in here? Money?" He knew from Monsignor Renton that the envelope contained money, but he hadn't told the Bishop, and so it probably sounded rash to him. Father Udovic could feel the Bishop disapproving of him, and Mrs. Anton still hadn't answered the question.

"Maybe you should return the envelope to Mrs. Anton, Father," said the Bishop.

That did it for Mrs. Anton. "It's got a dollar in it," she said.

Father Udovic glanced at the Bishop. The Bishop was adjusting his cuffs. This was something he did at funerals and public gatherings. It meant that things had gone on too long. Father Udovic's fingers were sticking to the envelope. He still couldn't believe it. "Feels like there's more than that," he said.

"I wrapped it up good in paper."

"You didn't write a letter or anything?"

"Was I supposed to?"

Father Udovic came down on her. "You were supposed to do what everybody else did. You were supposed to use the envelopes we had printed up for the purpose." He went back a few steps in his mind. "You told Monsignor Renton what was in the envelope?"

"Yes."

"Did you tell him how much?"

"No."

"Why not?"

"*He* didn't ask me."

And *he* didn't have to, thought Father Udovic. One look at Mrs. Anton and Monsignor Renton would know. Parish priests got to know such things. They were like weight-guessers, for whom it was only a question of ounces. Monsignor Renton shouldn't have passed Mrs. Anton on. He had opposed the plan to personalize Peter's Pence, but who would have thought he'd go to such lengths to get even with Father Udovic? It was sabotage. Father Udovic held out the envelope and pointed to the *Personal* on it. "What do you mean by that?" Here was where the creatures of his dreams had always gone away. He leaned forward for the answer.

Mrs. Anton leaned forward to give it. "I mean I don't want somebody else takin' all the credit with the Holy Father!"

Father Udovic sank back. It had been bad before, when she'd ignored him, but now it was worse. She was attacking the Bishop. If there were only a way to *prove* she was out of her mind, if only she'd say something that would make all her remarks acceptable in retrospect . . . "How's the Holy Father gonna know who this dollar came from if you didn't write anything?"

"I wrote my name and address on it. In ink."

"All right, Father," said the Bishop. He stood up and almost went out of the room before he stopped and looked back at Mrs. Anton. "Why don't you send it by regular mail?"

"He'd never see it! That's why! Some flunky'd get hold of it! Same as here! Oh, don't I know!"

The Bishop walked out, leaving them together—with the envelope.

In the next few moments, although Father Udovic knew

he had an obligation to instruct Mrs. Anton, and had the text for it—"When thou dost an alms-deed, sound not a trumpet before thee"—he despaired. He realized that they had needed each other to arrive at their sorry state. It seemed to him, sitting there saying nothing, that they saw each other as two people who'd sinned together on earth might see each other in hell, unchastened even then, only blaming each other for what had happened.

DEATH OF A FAVORITE

I had spent most of the afternoon mousing—a matter of sport with me and certainly not of diet—in the sunburnt fields that begin at our back door and continue hundreds of miles into the Dakotas. I gradually gave up the idea of hunting, the grasshoppers convincing me that there was no percentage in stealth. Even to doze was difficult, under such conditions, but I must have managed it. At least I was late coming to dinner, and so my introduction to the two missionaries took place at table. They were surprised, as most visitors are, to see me take the chair at Father Malt's right.

Father Malt, breaking off the conversation (if it could be called that), was his usual dear old self. "Fathers," he said, "meet Fritz."

I gave the newcomers the first good look that invariably tells me whether or not a person cares for cats. The mean old buck in charge of the team did not like me, I could see, and would bear watching. The other one obviously did like me, but he did not appear to be long enough from the seminary to matter. I felt that I had broken something less than even here.

"My assistant," said Father Malt, meaning me, and thus un-

24

consciously dealing out our fat friend at the other end of the
table. Poor Burner! There was a time when, thinking of him,
as I did now, as the enemy, I could have convinced myself
I meant something else. But he *is* the enemy, and I was right
from the beginning, when it could only have been instinct
that told me how much he hated me even while trying (in
his fashion!) to be friendly. (I believe his prejudice to be
acquired rather than congenital, and very likely, at this stage,
confined to me, not to cats as a class—there *is* that in his favor.
I intend to be fair about this if it kills me.)

My observations of humanity incline me to believe that one
of us—Burner or I—must ultimately prevail over the other. For
myself, I should not fear if this were a battle to be won on
the solid ground of Father Malt's affections. But the old man
grows older, the grave beckons to him ahead, and with Burner
pushing him from behind, how long can he last? Which is
to say: How long can *I* last? Unfortunately, it is naked power
that counts most in any rectory, and as things stand now, I
am safe only so long as Father Malt retains it here. Could I—
this impossible thought is often with me now—could I effect
a reconciliation and alliance with Father Burner? Impossible!
Yes, doubtless. But the question better asked is: *How* impossible? (Lord knows I would not inflict this line of reasoning
upon myself if I did not hold with the rumors that Father
Burner will be the one to succeed to the pastorate.) For I do
like it here. It is not at all in my nature to forgive and forget,
certainly not as regards Father Burner, but it is in my nature
to come to terms (much as nations do) when necessary, and
in this solution there need not be a drop of good will. No dog
can make that statement, or take the consequences, which I
understand are most serious, in the world to come. Shifts and
ententes. There is something fatal about the vocation of favorite, but it is the only one that suits me, and, all things con-

sidered—to dig I am not able, to beg I am ashamed—the rewards are adequate.

"We go through Chicago all the time," said the boss missionary, who seemed to be returning to a point he had reached when I entered. I knew Father Malt would be off that evening for a convention in Chicago. The missionaries, who would fill in for him and conduct forty hours' devotion on the side, belonged to an order just getting started in the diocese and were anxious to make a good impression. For the present, at least, as a kind of special introductory offer, they could be had dirt-cheap. Thanks to them, pastors who'd never been able to get away had got a taste of Florida last winter.

"Sometimes we stay over in Chicago," bubbled the young missionary. He was like a rookie ballplayer who hadn't made many road trips.

"We've got a house there," said the first, whose name in religion, as they say, was—so help me—Philbert. Later, Father Burner would get around it by calling him by his surname. Father Malt was the sort who wouldn't see anything funny about "Philbert," but it would be too much to expect him to remember such a name.

"What kind of a house?" asked Father Malt. He held up his hearing aid and waited for clarification.

Father Philbert replied in a shout, "The Order owns *a house* there!"

Father Malt fingered his hearing aid.

Father Burner sought to interpret for Father Philbert. "I think, Father, he wants to know what it's made out of."

"Red brick—it's red brick," bellowed Father Philbert.

"*My* house is red brick," said Father Malt.

"I *noticed* that," said Father Philbert.

Father Malt shoved the hearing aid at him.

"I know it," said Father Philbert, shouting again.

Father Malt nodded and fed me a morsel of fish. Even for a Friday, it wasn't much of a meal. I would not have been sorry to see this housekeeper go.

"All right, all right," said Father Burner to the figure lurking behind the door and waiting for him, always the last one, to finish. "She stands and looks in at you through the crack," he beefed. "Makes you feel like a condemned man." The housekeeper came into the room, and he addressed the young missionary (Burner was a great one for questioning the young): "Ever read any books by this fella Koestler, Father?"

"The Jesuit?" the young one asked.

"Hell, no, he's some kind of a writer. I know the man you mean, though. Spells his name different. Wrote a book—apologetics."

"That's the one. Very—"

"Dull."

"Well . . ."

"This other fella's not bad. He's a writer who's ahead of his time—about fifteen minutes. Good on jails and concentration camps. You'd think he was born in one if you ever read his books." Father Burner regarded the young missionary with absolute indifference. "But you didn't."

"No. Is he a Catholic?" inquired the young one.

"He's an Austrian or something."

"Oh."

The housekeeper removed the plates and passed the dessert around. When she came to Father Burner, he asked her privately, "What is it?"

"Pudding," she said, not whispering, as he would have liked.

"*Bread* pudding?" Now he was threatening her.

"Yes, Father."

Father Burner shuddered and announced to everybody, "No dessert for me." When the housekeeper had retired into the kitchen, he said, "Sometimes I think he got her from a hospital and sometimes, Father, I think she came from one of *your* fine institutions"—this to the young missionary.

Father Philbert, however, was the one to see the joke, and he laughed.

"My God," said Father Burner, growing bolder, "I'll never forget the time I stayed at your house in Louisville. If I hadn't been there for just a day—for the Derby, in fact—I'd have gone to Rome about it. I think I've had better meals here."

At the other end of the table, Father Malt, who could not have heard a word, suddenly blinked and smiled; the missionaries looked at him for some comment, in vain.

"He doesn't hear me," said Father Burner. "Besides, I think he's listening to the news."

"I didn't realize it was a radio too," said the young missionary.

"Oh, hell, yes."

"I think he's pulling your leg," said Father Philbert.

"Well, I thought so," said the young missionary ruefully.

"It's an idea," said Father Burner. Then in earnest to Father Philbert, whom he'd really been working around to all the time—the young one was decidedly not his type—"You the one drivin' that new Olds, Father?"

"It's not mine, Father," said Father Philbert with a meekness that would have been hard to take if he'd meant it. Father Burner understood him perfectly, however, and I thought they were two persons who would get to know each other a lot better.

"Nice job. They say it compares with the Cad in power. What do you call that color—oxford or clerical gray?"

"I really couldn't say, Father. It's my brother's. He's a layman in Minneapolis—St. Stephen's parish. He loaned it to me for this little trip."

Father Burner grinned. He could have been thinking, as I was, that Father Philbert protested too much. "Thought I saw you go by earlier," he said. "What's the matter—didn't you want to come in when you saw the place?"

Father Philbert, who was learning to ignore Father Malt, laughed discreetly. "Couldn't be sure this was it. That house on the *other* side of the church, now—"

Father Burner nodded. "Like that, huh? Belongs to a Mason."

Father Philbert sighed and said, "It would."

"Not at all," said Father Burner. "I like 'em better than K.C.s." If he could get the audience for it, Father Burner enjoyed being broad-minded. Gazing off in the direction of the Mason's big house, he said, "I've played golf with him."

The young missionary looked at Father Burner in horror. Father Philbert merely smiled. Father Burner, toying with a large crumb, propelled it in my direction.

"Did a bell ring?" asked Father Malt.

"His P.A. system," Father Burner explained. "Better tell him," he said to the young missionary. "You're closer. He can't bring me in on those batteries he uses."

"No bell," said the young missionary, lapsing into basic English and gestures.

Father Malt nodded, as though he hadn't really thought so.

"How do you like it?" said Father Burner.

Father Philbert hesitated, and then he said, "Here, you mean?"

"I wouldn't ask you that," said Father Burner, laughing. "Talkin' about that Olds. Like it? Like the Hydramatic?"

"No kiddin', Father. It's not mine," Father Philbert protested.

"All right, all right," said Father Burner, who obviously did not believe him. "Just so you don't bring up your vow of poverty." He looked at Father Philbert's uneaten bread pudding—"Had enough?"—and rose from the table, blessing himself. The other two followed when Father Malt, who was feeding me cheese, waved them away. Father Burner came around to us, bumping my chair—intentionally, I know. He stood behind Father Malt and yelled into his ear, "Any calls for me this aft?" He'd been out somewhere, as usual. I often thought he expected too much to happen in his absence.

"There was something . . ." said Father Malt, straining his memory, which was poor.

"Yes?"

"Now I remember—they had the wrong number."

Father Burner, looking annoyed and downhearted, left the room.

"They said they'd call back," said Father Malt, sensing Father Burner's disappointment.

I left Father Malt at the table reading his Office under the orange light of the chandelier. I went to the living room, to my spot in the window from which I could observe Father Burner and the missionaries on the front porch, the young one in the swing with his breviary—the mosquitoes, I judged, were about to join him—and the other two just smoking and standing around, like pool players waiting for a table. I heard Father Philbert say, "Like to take a look at it, Father?"

"Say, that's an idea," said Father Burner.

I saw them go down the front walk to the gray Olds parked at the curb. With Father Burner at the wheel they drove away. In a minute they were back, the car moving uncertainly—this I noted with considerable pleasure until I realized that Father Burner was simply testing the brakes. Then they were gone, and after a bit, when they did not return, I supposed they were out killing poultry on the open road.

30

That evening, when the ushers dropped in at the rectory, there was not the same air about them as when they came for pinochle. Without fanfare, Mr. Bauman, their leader, who had never worked any but the center aisle, presented Father Malt with a traveling bag. It was nice of him, I thought, when he said, "It's from all of us," for it could not have come from all equally. Mr. Bauman, in hardware, and Mr. Keller, the druggist, were the only ones well off, and must have forked out plenty for such a fine piece of luggage, even after the discount.

Father Malt thanked all six ushers with little nods in which there was no hint of favoritism. "Ha," he kept saying. "You shouldn'a done it."

The ushers bobbed and ducked, dodging his flattery, and kept up a mumble to the effect that Father Malt deserved everything they'd ever done for him and more. Mr. Keller came forward to instruct Father Malt in the use of the various clasps and zippers. Inside the bag was another gift, a set of military brushes, which I could see they were afraid he would not discover for himself. But he unsnapped a brush, and, like the veteran crowd-pleaser he was, swiped once or twice at his head with it after spitting into the bristles. The ushers all laughed.

"Pretty snazzy," said the newest usher—the only young blood among them. Mr. Keller had made him a clerk at the store, had pushed through his appointment as alternate usher in the church, and was gradually weaning him away from his motorcycle. With Mr. Keller, the lad formed a block to Mr. Bauman's power, but he was perhaps worse than no ally at all. Most of the older men, though they pretended a willingness to help him meet the problems of an usher, were secretly pleased when he bungled at collection time and skipped a row or overlapped one.

Mr. Keller produced a box of ten-cent cigars, which, as a *personal* gift from him, came as a bitter surprise to the others. He was not big enough, either, to attribute it to them too. He had anticipated their resentment, however, and now produced a bottle of milk of magnesia. No one could deny the comic effect, for Father Malt had been known to recommend the blue bottle from the confessional.

"Ha!" said Father Malt, and everybody laughed.

"In case you get upset on the trip," said the druggist.

"You know it's the best thing," said Father Malt in all seriousness, and then even he remembered he'd said it too often before. He passed the cigars. The box went from hand to hand, but, except for the druggist's clerk, nobody would have one.

Father Malt, seeing this, wisely renewed his thanks for the bag, insisting upon his indebtedness until it was actually in keeping with the idea the ushers had of their own generosity. Certainly none of them had ever owned a bag like that. Father Malt went to the housekeeper with it and asked her to transfer his clothes from the old bag, already packed, to the new one. When he returned, the ushers were still standing around feeling good about the bag and not so good about the cigars. They'd discuss that later. Father Malt urged them to sit down. He seemed to want them near him as long as possible. They *were* his friends, but I could not blame Father Burner for avoiding them. He was absent now, as he usually managed to be when the ushers called. If he ever succeeded Father Malt, who let them have the run of the place, they would be the first to suffer—after me! As Father Malt was the heart, they were the substance of a parish that remained rural while becoming increasingly suburban. They dressed up occasionally and dropped into St. Paul and Minneapolis, "the Cities," as visiting firemen into hell, though it would be difficult to imagine any other place as graceless and far-gone as our own hard little highway town—called Sherwood but about as sylvan as a tennis court.

They were regular fellows—not so priestly as their urban colleagues—loud, heavy of foot, wearers of long underwear in wintertime and iron-gray business suits the year round. Their idea of a good time (pilsener beer, cheap cigars smoked with the bands left on, and pinochle) coincided nicely with their understanding of "doing good" (a percentage of every pot went to the parish building fund). Their wives, also active, played cards in the church basement and sold vanilla extract and chances--mostly to each other, it appeared—with all the revenue over cost going to what was known as "the missions." This evening I could be grateful that time was not going to permit the usual pinochle game. (In the midst of all their pounding—almost as hard on me as it was on the dining-room table—I often felt they should have played on a meat block.)

The ushers, settling down all over the living room, started to talk about Father Malt's trip to Chicago. The housekeeper brought in a round of beer.

"How long you be gone, Father—three days?" one of them asked.

Father Malt said that he'd be gone about three days.

"Three days! This is Friday. Tomorrow's Saturday. Sunday. Monday." Everything stopped while the youngest usher counted on his fingers. "Back on Tuesday?"

Father Malt nodded.

"Who's takin' over on Sunday?"

Mr. Keller answered for Father Malt. "He's got some missionary fathers in."

"Missionaries!"

The youngest usher then began to repeat himself on one of his two or three topics. "Hey, Father, don't forget to drop in the U.S.O. if it's still there. I was in Chi during the war," he said, but nobody would listen to him.

Mr. Bauman had cornered Father Malt and was trying to tell him where that place was—that place where he'd eaten his meals during the World's Fair; one of the waitresses was from Minnesota. I'd had enough of this—the next thing would be a diagram on the back of an envelope—and I'd heard Father Burner come in earlier. I went upstairs to check on him. For a minute or two I stood outside his room listening. He had Father Philbert with him, and, just as I'd expected, he was talking against Father Malt, leading up to the famous question with which Father Malt, years ago, had received the Sherwood appointment from the Archbishop: "Have dey got dere a goot meat shop?"

Father Philbert laughed, and I could hear him sip from his glass and place it on the floor beside his chair. I entered the room, staying close to the baseboard, in the shadows, curious to know what they were drinking. I maneuvered myself into position to sniff Father Philbert's glass. To my surprise, scotch. Here was proof that Father Burner considered Father Philbert a friend. At that moment I could not think what it was he expected to get out of a lowly missionary. My mistake, not realizing then how correct and prophetic I'd been earlier in thinking of them as two of a kind. It seldom happened that Father Burner got out the real scotch for company, or for himself *in* company. For most guests he had nothing—a safe policy, since a surprising number of temperance cranks passed through the rectory—and for unwelcome guests who would like a drink he kept a bottle of "scotch-type" whiskey, which was a smooth, smoky blend of furniture polish that came in a fancy bottle, was offensive even when watered, and cheap, though rather hard to get since the end of the war. He had a charming way of plucking the rare bottle from a bureau drawer, as if this were indeed an occasion for him; even so, he would not touch the stuff, presenting himself as a chap of simple tastes, of no taste at all for the things of this world, who would prefer, if anything, the rude wine made from our own grapes—if we'd had any grapes. Quite an act, and one he thoroughly enjoyed, holding his glass of pure water and asking, "How's your drink, Father? Strong enough?"

The housekeeper, appearing at the door, said there'd been a change of plans and some of the ushers were driving Father Malt to the train.

"Has he gone yet?" asked Father Burner.

"Not yet, Father."

"Well, tell him good-by for me."

"Yes, Father."

When she had gone, he said, "I'd tell him myself, but I don't want to run into that bunch."

Father Philbert smiled. "What's he up to in Chicago?"

"They've got one of those pastors' and builders' conventions going on at the Stevens Hotel."

"Is he building?"

"No, but he's a pastor and he'll get a lot of free samples. He won't buy anything."

"Not much has been done around here, huh?" said Father Philbert.

He had fed Father Burner the question he wanted. "He built that fish pond in the back yard—for his minnows. That's the extent of the building program in his time. Of course he's only been here a while."

"How long?"

"Fourteen years," said Father Burner. *He* would be the greatest builder of them all—if he ever got the chance. He lit a cigarette and smiled. "What he's really going to Chicago for is to see a couple of ball games."

Father Philbert did not smile. "Who's playing there now?" he said.

A little irritated at this interest, Father Burner said, "I believe it's the Red Sox—or is it the Reds? Hell, how do I know?"

"Couldn't be the Reds," said Father Philbert. "The boy and I were in Cincinnati last week and it was the start of a long home stand for them."

"Very likely," said Father Burner.

While the missionary, a Cardinal fan, analyzed the pennant race in the National League, Father Burner sulked. "What's the best train out of Chicago for Washington?" he suddenly inquired.

Father Philbert told him what he could, but admitted that his information dated from some years back. "We don't make the run to Washington any more."

"That's right," said Father Burner. "Washington's in the American League."

Father Philbert laughed, turning aside the point that he traveled with the Cardinals. "I thought you didn't know about these things," he said.

"About these things it's impossible to stay ignorant," said Father Burner. "Here, and the last place, and the place before that, and in the seminary—a ball, a bat, and God. I'll be damned, Father, if I'll do as the Romans do."

"What price glory?" inquired Father Philbert, as if he smelt heresy.

"I know," said Father Burner. "And it'll probably cost me the red hat." A brave comment, perhaps, from a man not yet a country pastor, and it showed me where his thoughts were again. He did not disguise his humble ambition by speaking lightly of an impossible one. "Scratch a prelate and you'll find a second baseman," he fumed.

Father Philbert tried to change the subject. "Somebody told me Father Malt's the exorcist for the diocese."

"Used to be." Father Burner's eyes flickered balefully.

"Overdid it, huh?" asked Father Philbert—as if he hadn't heard!

"Some." I expected Father Burner to say more. He could have told some pretty wild stories, the gist of them all that Father Malt, as an exorcist, was perhaps a little quick on the trigger. He had stuck pretty much to livestock, however, which was to his credit in the human view.

"Much scandal?"

"Some."

"Nothing serious, though?"

"No."

"Suppose it depends on what you call serious."

Father Burner did not reply. He had become oddly morose. Perhaps he felt that he was being catered to out of pity, or that Father Philbert, in giving him so many opportunities to talk against Father Malt, was tempting him.

"Who plays the accordion?" inquired Father Philbert, hearing it downstairs.

"He does."

"Go on!"

"Sure."

"How can he hear what he's playing?"

"What's the difference—if he plays an accordion?"

Father Philbert laughed. He removed the cellophane from a cigar, and then he saw me. And at that moment I made no attempt to hide. "There's that damn cat."

"His assistant!" said Father Burner with surprising bitterness. "Coadjutor with right of succession."

Father Philbert balled up the cellophane and tossed it at the wastebasket, missing.

"Get it," he said to me fatuously.

I ignored him, walking slowly toward the door.

Father Burner made a quick movement with his feet, which were something to behold, but I knew he wouldn't get up, and took my sweet time.

Father Philbert inquired, "Will she catch mice?"

She! Since coming to live at the rectory, I've been celibate, it's true, but I daresay I'm as manly as the next one. And Father Burner, who might have done me the favor of putting him straight, said nothing.

"She looks pretty fat to be much of a mouser."

I just stared at the poor man then, as much as to say that I'd think one so interested in catching mice would have heard of a little thing called the mousetrap. After one last dirty look, I left them to themselves—to punish each other with their company.

I strolled down the hall, trying to remember when I'd last had a mouse. Going past the room occupied by the young missionary, I smiled upon his door, which was shut, confident that he was inside hard at his prayers.

The next morning, shortly after breakfast, which I took, as usual, in the kitchen, I headed for the cool orchard, to which I often repaired on just such a day as this one promised to be. I had no appetite for the sparrows hopping from tree to tree above me, but there seemed no way to convince them of that. Each one, so great is his vanity, thinks himself eminently edible. Peace, peace, they cry, and there is no peace. Finally, tired of their noise, I got up from the matted grass and left, leveling my ears and flailing my tail, in a fake dudgeon that inspired the males to feats of stunt flying and terrorized the young females most delightfully.

I went then to another favorite spot of mine, that bosky

Death of a Favorite

strip of green between the church and the brick sidewalk. Here, however, the horseflies found me, and as if that were not enough, visions of stray dogs and children came between me and the kind of sleep I badly needed after an uncommonly restless night.

When afternoon came, I remembered that it was Saturday, and that I could have the rectory to myself. Father Burner and the missionaries would be busy with confessions. By this time the temperature had reached its peak, and though I felt sorry for the young missionary, I must admit the thought of the other two sweltering in the confessionals refreshed me. The rest of the afternoon I must have slept something approaching the sleep of the just.

I suppose it was the sound of dishes that roused me. I rushed into the dining room, not bothering to wash up, and took my customary place at the table. Only then did I consider the empty chair next to me—the utter void. This, I thought, is a foreshadowing of what I must someday face—this, and Father Burner munching away at the other end of the table. And there was the immediate problem: no one to serve me. The young missionary smiled at me, but how can you eat a smile? The other two, looking rather wilted—to their hot boxes I wished them swift return—talked in expiring tones of reserved sins and did not appear to notice me. Our first meal together without Father Malt did not pass without incident, however. It all came about when the young missionary extended a thin sliver of meat to me.

"Hey, don't do that!" said Father Philbert. "You'll never make a mouser out of her that way."

Father Burner, too, regarded the young missionary with disapproval.

"Just this one piece," said the young missionary. The meat was already in my mouth.

"Well, watch it in the future," said Father Philbert. It was the word "future" that worried me. Did it mean that he had arranged to cut off my sustenance in the kitchen too? Did it mean that until Father Malt returned I had to choose between mousing and fasting?

I continued to think along these melancholy lines until the repast, which had never begun for me, ended for them. Then I whisked into the kitchen, where I received the usual bowl of milk. But whether the housekeeper, accustomed as she was to having me eat my main course at table, assumed there had been no change in my life, or was now acting under instructions from these villains, I don't know. I was too sickened by their meanness to have any appetite. When the pastor's away, the curates will play, I thought. On the whole I was feeling pretty glum.

It was our custom to have the main meal at noon on Sundays. I arrived early, before the others, hungrier than I'd been for as long as I could remember, and still I had little or no expectation of food at this table. I was there for one purpose—to assert myself—and possibly, where the young missionary was concerned, to incite sympathy for myself and contempt for my persecutors. By this time I knew that to be the name for them.

They entered the dining room, just the two of them.

"Where's the kid?" asked Father Burner.

"He's not feeling well," said Father Philbert.

I was not surprised. They'd arranged between the two of them to have him say the six and eleven o'clock Masses, which meant, of course, that he'd fasted in the interval. I had not thought of him as the hardy type, either.

"I'll have the housekeeper take him some beef broth," said Father Burner. Damned white of you, I was thinking, when he suddenly whirled and swept me off my chair. Then he picked it up and placed it against the wall. Then he went to the lower end of the table, removed his plate and silverware, and brought them to Father Malt's place. Talking and fuming to himself, he sat down in Father Malt's chair. I did not appear very brave, I fear, cowering under mine.

Father Philbert, who had been watching with interest, now greeted the new order with a cheer. "Attaboy, Ernest!"

Father Burner began to justify himself. "More light here," he said, and added, "Cats kill birds," and for some reason he was puffing.

"If they'd just kill mice," said Father Philbert, "they wouldn't be so bad." He had a one-track mind if I ever saw one.

"Wonder how many that black devil's caught in his time?" said Father Burner, airing a common prejudice against cats of my shade (though I do have a white collar). He looked over at me. "Sssss," he said. But I held my ground.

"I'll take a dog any day," said the platitudinous Father Philbert.

"Me, too."

After a bit, during which time they played hard with the roast, Father Philbert said, "How about taking her for a ride in the country?"

"Hell," said Father Burner, "he'd just come back."

"Not if we did it right, she wouldn't."

"Look," said Father Burner. "Some friends of mine dropped a cat off the high bridge in St. Paul. They saw him go under in mid-channel. I'm talking about the Mississippi, understand. Thought they'd never lay eyes on that animal again. That's what they thought. He was back at the house before they were." Father Burner paused—he could see that he was not convincing Father Philbert—and then he tried again. "That's a fact, Father. They might've played a quick round of golf

41

before they got back. Cat didn't even look damp, they said. He's still there. Case a lot like this. Except now they're afraid of *him*."

To Father Burner's displeasure, Father Philbert refused to be awed or even puzzled. He simply inquired, "But did they use a bag? Weights?"

"Millstones," snapped Father Burner. "Don't quibble."

Then they fell to discussing the burial customs of gangsters—poured concrete and the rest—and became so engrossed in the matter that they forgot all about me.

Over against the wall, I was quietly working up the courage to act against them. When I felt sufficiently lionhearted, I leaped up and occupied my chair. Expecting blows and vilification, I encountered only indifference. I saw then how far I'd come down in their estimation. Already the remembrance of things past—the disease of noble politicals in exile—was too strong in me, the hope of restoration unwarrantably faint.

At the end of the meal, returning to me, Father Philbert remarked, "I think I know a better way." Rising, he snatched the crucifix off the wall, passed it to a bewildered Father Burner, and, saying "Nice Kitty," grabbed me behind the ears. "Hold it up to her," said Father Philbert. Father Burner held the crucifix up to me. "See that?" said Father Philbert to my face. I miaowed. "Take that!" said Father Philbert, cuffing me. He pushed my face into the crucifix again. "See that?" he said again, but I knew what to expect next, and when he cuffed me, I went for his hand with my mouth, pinking him nicely on the wrist. Evidently Father Burner had begun to understand and appreciate the proceedings. Although I was in a good position to observe everything, I could not say as much for myself. "Association," said Father Burner with mysterious satisfaction, almost with zest. He poked the crucifix at me. "If he's just smart enough to react properly," he said.

"Oh, she's plenty smart," said Father Philbert, sucking his wrist and giving himself, I hoped, hydrophobia. He scuffed off one of his sandals for a paddle. Father Burner, fingering the crucifix nervously, inquired, "Sure it's all right to go on with this thing?" "It's the intention that counts in these things," said Father Philbert. "Our motive is clear enough." And they went at me again.

After that first taste of the sandal in the dining room, I foolishly believed I would be safe as long as I stayed away from the table; there was something about my presence there, I thought, that brought out the beast in them—which is to say very nearly all that was in them. But they caught me in the upstairs hall the same evening, one brute thundering down upon me, the other sealing off my only avenue of escape. And this beating was worse than the first—preceded as it was by a short delay that I mistook for a reprieve until Father Burner, who had gone downstairs muttering something about "leaving no margin for error," returned with the crucifix from the dining room, although we had them hanging all over the house. The young missionary, coming upon them while they were at me, turned away. "I wash my hands of it," he said. I thought he might have done more.

Out of mind, bruised of body, sick at heart, for two days and nights I held on, I know not how or why—unless I lived in hope of vengeance. I wanted simple justice, a large order in itself, but I would never have settled for that alone. I wanted nothing less than my revenge.

I kept to the neighborhood, but avoided the rectory. I believed, of course, that their only strategy was to drive me away. I derived some little satisfaction from making myself scarce, for it was thus I deceived them into thinking their plan to banish me successful. But this was my single comfort during this hard time, and it was as nothing against their crimes.

I spent the nights in the open fields. I reeled, dizzy with hunger, until I bagged an aged field mouse. It tasted bitter to me, this stale provender, and seemed, as I swallowed it, an ironic concession to the enemy. I vowed I'd starve before I ate another mouse. By way of retribution to myself, I stalked sparrows in the orchard—hating myself for it but persisting all the more when I thought of those bird-lovers, my persecutors, before whom I could stand and say in self-redemption, "You made me what I am now. You thrust the killer's part upon me." Fortunately, I did not flush a single sparrow. Since *my* motive was clear enough, however, I'd had the pleasure of sinning against them and their ideals, the pleasure without the feathers and mess.

On Tuesday, the third day, all caution, I took up my post in the lilac bush beside the garage. Not until Father Malt returned, I knew, would I be safe in daylight. He arrived along about dinnertime, and I must say the very sight of him aroused a sentiment in me akin to human affection. The youngest usher, who must have had the afternoon off to meet him at the station in St. Paul, carried the new bag before him into the rectory. It was for me an act symbolic of the counter-revolution to come. I did not rush out from my hiding place, however. I had suffered too much to play the fool now. Instead I slipped into the kitchen by way of the flap in the screen door, which they had not thought to barricade. I waited under the stove for my moment, like an actor in the wings.

Presently I heard them tramping into the dining room and seating themselves, and Father Malt's voice saying, "I had a long talk with the Archbishop." (I could almost hear Father Burner praying, Did he say anything about *me?*) And then, "Where's Fritz?"

"He hasn't been around lately," said Father Burner cunningly. He would not tell the truth and he would not tell a lie.

"You know, there's something mighty funny about that cat," said Father Philbert. "We think she's possessed."

I was astonished, and would have liked a moment to think it over, but by now I was already entering the room.

"*Possessed!*" said Father Malt. "Aw, no!"

"Ah, yes," said Father Burner, going for the meat right away. "And good riddance."

And then I miaowed and they saw me.

"Quick!" said Father Philbert, who made a nice recovery after involuntarily reaching for me and his sandal at the same time. Father Burner ran to the wall for the crucifix, which had been, until now, a mysterious and possibly blasphemous feature of my beatings—the crucifix held up to me by the one not scourging at the moment, as if it were the will behind my punishment. They had schooled me well, for even now, at the sight of the crucifix, an undeniable fear was rising in me. Father Burner handed it to Father Malt.

"Now you'll see," said Father Philbert.

"We'll leave it up to you," said Father Burner.

I found now that I could not help myself. What followed was hidden from them—from human eyes. I gave myself over entirely to the fear they'd beaten into me, and in a moment, according to their plan, I was fleeing the crucifix as one truly possessed, out of the dining room and into the kitchen, and from there, blindly, along the house and through the shrubbery, ending in the street, where a powerful gray car ran over me— and where I gave up the old ghost for a new one.

Simultaneously, reborn, redeemed from my previous fear, identical with my former self, so far as they could see, and still in their midst, I padded up to Father Malt—he still sat gripping the crucifix—and jumped into his lap. I heard the

45

young missionary arriving from an errand in Father Philbert's *brother's* car, late for dinner he thought, but just in time to see the stricken look I saw coming into the eyes of my persecutors. This look alone made up for everything I'd suffered at their hands. Purring now, I was rubbing up against the crucifix, myself effecting my utter revenge.

"What have we done?" cried Father Philbert. He was basically an emotional dolt and would have voted then for my canonization.

"I ran over a cat!" said the young missionary excitedly. "I'd swear it was this one. When I looked, there was nothing there!"

"Better go upstairs and rest," growled Father Burner. He sat down—it was good to see him in his proper spot at the low end of the table—as if to wait a long time, or so it seemed to me. I found myself wondering if I could possibly bring about his transfer to another parish—one where they had a devil for a pastor and several assistants, where he would be able to start at the bottom again.

But first things first, I always say, and all in good season, for now Father Malt himself was drawing my chair up to the table, restoring me to my rightful place.

THE POOR THING

Her pension from the store wasn't enough. She tried to conceal this from Mrs. Shepherd, saying she *preferred* to be doing something, but knew she sounded like a person in need of a job, and she had, after all, come to an employment agency. Mrs. Shepherd, however, found a word for it. "Oh, you mean you want to *supplement* your income." And to that Teresa could agree.

The next day Mrs. Shepherd called. She was in a spot, she said, or she wouldn't ask Teresa to consider what she had to offer. It wasn't the kind of position Teresa was down for, but perhaps she'd accept it on a temporary basis.

"You know, Mrs. Shepherd, I don't *have* to work."

"My dear, I know you don't. You just want to supplement your income."

"Yes, and I like to be doing something."

"My dear, I know how you feel."

"And I'm down for light sewing."

"Of course you are. I don't know what ever made me think of you for this—except they want a nice refined person that's a Catholic."

Teresa, dreaming over the compliment, heard Mrs. Shepherd

say, "This party isn't offering enough. In fact, I hate to tell you what it is. Say, I wonder if you'd just let me call them back and maybe I can get you more money. If I can't, I don't want you to even consider it. How's that?"

"Well, all right," Teresa said, "but I don't have to work."

When Mrs. Shepherd called again, Teresa said it wasn't very much money and not in her line at all and would not be persuaded—until Mrs. Shepherd said something indirectly about their friendship.

The next morning Teresa got on the streetcar and rode out into the suburbs. Mrs. Shepherd had referred to Teresa's charge-to-be as a semi-invalid. The poor thing who met Teresa at the door in a wheel chair wore an artificial flower in her artificial hair, but had the face of a child, small, sweet, gay. Her name was Dorothy. She had always been Dolly to everybody, however, and it did seem to fit her.

Teresa could truthfully say to Mrs. Shepherd, who called up that evening to ask how things were going, that the poor dear was no trouble at all, neat as a pin, nice as you please, and that they were already calling each other by their first names. Mrs. Shepherd was glad to hear it, she said, but she hadn't forgotten that Teresa was down for light sewing. Teresa only had to say the word if she wanted to make a change.

Teresa's duties were those of a companion. She went home at night, and had Saturdays and Sundays off. Dolly's sister, a teacher, got breakfast in the morning and was home in time to prepare dinner. For lunch, Teresa served green tea, cinnamon toast, and a leafy vegetable. Over Dolly's protests, she did some house cleaning. At first Dolly tried to help. Then she tried to get Teresa to give it up and listen to the radio.

That was how Dolly spent the day, dialing from memory, charting her course at fifteen-minute intervals, from Fred Waring in the morning to Morton Downey at night. In be-

48

tween came the dramatic programs tnat Teresa, as a working person, had scarcely known about. Dolly was a great one for writing in to the stations. She'd been in correspondence with CBS all during all the criminal trials of Lord Henry Brinthrop (of Black Swan Hall) in "Our Gal Sunday." She was one of those faithful listeners who plead with the networks to bring back deceased characters, but it wasn't the lovable ones who concerned her. She said some of the bad ones got off too easily, "just dying." One afternoon she chanced to dial to "Make Believe Ballroom," a program of popular recordings, and got the idea that it should include *some* sacred music. (After a week of constant listening, they heard the announcer read Dolly's letter and ask listeners for their views. Dolly, expecting trouble, wrote another letter, but that was the last they heard of her suggestion.)

They were getting to know each other. Dolly, who had always been an invalid, said she'd hoped in the past that something might be done for her. Now, however, she was resigned to God's will (she had visited St. Anne de Beaupré in Canada, where it had not been God's will to cure her, and Lourdes was too far and expensive), but, really, she wasn't to be pitied, she said, when you considered the poor souls in the "leopard colonies." The sufferings of the "leopards" were much with Dolly, and she sent them a dollar a month, wishing it might be more. They often discussed the leopards—too often to suit Teresa. Dolly had read a great deal about them and knew of the most frightful cases, which she told about, she said, to excite sympathy in herself and others. Teresa said she was having nightmares from hearing about the cases (in fact she wasn't). "Which one? Which one?" Dolly wanted to know, but Teresa wouldn't lie any more to her. Dolly said she was sorry. She didn't stop her awful stories, however.

Mrs. Shepherd called again. "Still getting along famously?"

Teresa, a little disturbed to hear Mrs. Shepherd speak of her as a party she'd "placed," which sounded so permanent, said that she had no complaints.

One rainy afternoon when it was so dark they should have had a light, and with the radio off on account of lightning, Dolly said, "Teresa, I consider you my best friend." For some reason Teresa was moved to say that she might have married. The first time she had been too young, or so she had been told, and the second time, also the last time, she had been living with some people who hadn't wanted her to leave them. They hadn't been relatives or close friends, or even friends until she moved in, just people with whom she'd roomed, that was all. Dolly seemed to understand. Teresa could not say that she did, now, but was grateful to Dolly for not scolding or ridiculing her—others had.

Dolly said, "If you'd got married, Teresa, just think—maybe you wouldn't be here today. Now tell me how you got your first raise at the store."

Dolly, for someone who liked to talk, was a good listener, though she occasionally missed the point, or discovered one that Teresa could never find. "You want to hear that again? I declare, Dolly, you're a funny one."

So Teresa told her again how she'd seen this notice in the paper that the store had declared a dividend and how she'd worried all night over what she knew she must do in the morning. The first thing, then, after hanging up her coat and hat, she went to the supervisor of the sewing room. The supervisor sat on an elevated chair, a kind of throne in that mean setting, and stared down on the girls below.

"How'd she look, Teresa?"

Teresa made the face she'd made the first time, now an indispensable feature of the story.

"What'd you do then, Teresa?"

"I said, 'If you please, Miss Merck, I see by the paper the store declared a dividend.'"

Dolly clapped her hands. "How'd she look then?"

"My lands, do I have to go through it all again?"

"Please."

Teresa made the face again.

"Then what?"

"I said, 'If the store can declare a dividend they ought to be able to pay me more than five dollars a week. It's not very much to live on.'"

Dolly crushed her hands to her face. "Oh, Teresa, you shouldn't have said it!"

"Of course," Teresa said, "that was years ago. They have to pay good now."

"Go on, Teresa."

Now Miss Merck was getting down from her throne and directing Teresa to follow her into the cloakroom.

"Oh, oh," Dolly said. "Now you're gonna catch it."

"I thought she was going to show me the door."

"Show me how she walked, Teresa."

Teresa stood up and did a slow goose step across the room.

"Oh, Lord, Teresa! Don't I pity you!"

Teresa growled a little, which was not in the original Miss Merck, or even in the part as she'd previously played it for Dolly, and it was a great success. Dolly swooned, her head toppling back on her pillow, her eyes closed against the reality of Miss Merck, but still peeking. When she had recovered, Teresa continued—as Miss Merck herself:

"Girl, you're a poor hand with a needle!"

"Oh, you were not!" cried Dolly.

"Of course I wasn't," said Teresa, "but that was part of her game."

"No!"

"Oh, yes."

"Go on."

"Girl, how can you expect to be kept on at the present wage, let alone get a raise?"

"Oh, Teresa, you're gonna lose your job!"

"I'll admit I was going for my hat and coat," said Teresa, pausing to remember.

"Is that all?"

"You know it isn't."

"All right, Teresa."

"But"—and to Miss Merck's voice something nastier had been added—"sewing isn't everything. Do *I* sew, girl?"

"What'd she mean? What'd she mean?"

"You know what she meant. She came right out with it then. She wanted me to be her assistant, at seven dollars a week. And she said not to tell the other girls about the dividend."

"That's not all, Teresa. You're not telling it all."

"That's how I got my raise. That's what you asked to hear."

"Please, Teresa."

"All right—and when she died I got her job."

"*Died!*"

"Yes."

"You got her job when she died——?"

"Of cancer."

"*Cancer!*"

And now it was just as though they were back on the leopards, with Dolly telling how, one by one, their members fell off. For Teresa the story ended in the raise and promotion, not in her succession to the throne on Miss Merck's death or the cause of it.

"I'm glad I'm not a cancer person," Dolly would say when they were looking up birthdays in the almanac. Dolly was fascinated by the Crab in the zodiac, and by Leo, her sign, which reminded her of the early Christian martyrs. "I wouldn't be afraid to die that way, would you, Teresa?"

"I certainly would."

"So would *I!*"

Teresa made a mistake when she mentioned her brother and his family and the good time she'd had with them one summer, long ago, at a lake cottage. (She remembered telling her little niece and nephew that she'd like to be one of the cows they saw standing in a flooded meadow, and they'd thought she really meant it. They'd told strangers, in an eating place where they'd stopped, that their aunt wanted to be a cow. "Oh, no, Teresa," cried Dolly, going deeper into the matter. "And have some rough farmer . . .") The trouble was that Dolly was forever asking if the little drowning victims she read about weren't just the age of Teresa's little nephew or niece, and wasn't it a wonder they hadn't all drowned in Wisconsin? Teresa would snap, "They're grown-up now," or, "They don't go there any more."

Dolly gave Teresa a package for her niece and nephew one day, saying it was hard to find something that boys and girls both liked. She wouldn't tell Teresa what was in the package— it was a secret. "Hold it to your ear. Just tell them that. Say it a hundred times to yourself, Teresa, so you won't forget." When Teresa got home, she looked inside the package, and a good thing she had. All done up in tissue paper was an old sea shell, with a little card, "Your unknown friend, Dolly S." When Dolly asked how they'd liked the gift, Teresa said she hadn't given it to them yet. Finally, one day, tired of being asked about it, she said, "They liked it fine. They use it all the time."

Dolly was tight. She took the longest time rooting in her purse for the three cents she owed Teresa for a stamp. (She wanted Teresa to buy stamps one at a time, as if expecting the market to break, but Teresa secretly bought a supply and retailed them to Dolly as needed.) And one week Teresa paid the paper boy and never did get it back. Dolly hated the time when she must send her dollar to the leopards. "Well," she'd say, as if she were a woman in her first pregnancy, "it won't be long now." When the day arrived, sweat broke out all over the poor thing. "Oh, come on, cheer up," Teresa said about the third time this happened, and tossed a dollar into her lap.

Dolly would not take it, she said, taking it. She tried to swear Teresa to a like amount regularly, saying they could rotate the months, which came too often for one. "Pledge yourself, Teresa."

"I won't do it, not for you or anybody. And besides I may not be here."

"Oh, Teresa, don't say that!"

Then Dolly tried to convert Teresa to her special devotions. But Teresa was wary of coming under Dolly's spiritual guidance, embarrassed too at the thought of praying with anyone unless in church. When Dolly persisted, rattling off the indulgences to be gained here and there (she kept books and knew exactly how many days she had coming), Teresa said it was her privilege to worship as she pleased.

One Monday morning, when Dolly met Teresa at the front door, she held some little wads of paper in her outstretched hand.

"What's all this?"

"Go ahead and draw one, Teresa. See what you have to practice this week." Teresa drew one. Dolly, after shaking the wads like dice, opened her hand and selected one.

"What's yours, Teresa?"

" 'Kindness to others.' I can't read the rest."

"Is it 'Alms for the leopards'?"

"I guess it is. What's yours?"

Dolly sighed, " 'More prayers for the poor souls in purgatory.' "

In the ensuing weeks, Dolly's assignments all had to do with prayer, for a variety of beneficiaries, and Teresa was stuck with "kindness to others" and "alms." Dolly kept the extra wads on her person, and so Teresa had no opportunity to investigate the possibility of fraud. Dolly went on as though she had much the worst of it, and to hear her tell it, she didn't have a free minute from her prayers.

When Teresa gave a short answer, Dolly would remind her that she was supposed to be practicing kindness that week. Sometimes Dolly would ask the silliest questions.

"Do you smoke, Teresa?"

"Once in a while is all."

"Teresa! I know you don't. You don't look it."

"Then why'd you ask?"

"I don't call that kindness to others, Teresa."

Teresa, for her part, did not blame the priest for not coming every week to hear Dolly's confession, a principal complaint with her. Once, when he was there, Teresa had heard Dolly confess, "I missed my morning prayers two times, Father."

"Is that all?"

"Is that all!"

The next time Dolly complained about the priest's not coming often enough, Teresa said, "If you told him half the things you do, you wouldn't want him to come so often. You never think to tell him all those mean things you say about the woman across the way. Don't forget Our Lord was a Jew."

"Teresa! Our Lord was a Galilean. And remember what you're practicing this week."

When Dolly pouted, and she might if the programs were good enough to hold her, Teresa was glad for the rest. Too soon, she knew, Dolly would roll into the next room and start up some fool thing.

"Teresa, have your brother come out sometime and see where you work."

"Huh! I don't have to work. Why would he want to come 'way out here? He's got a nice place of his own."

"Hasn't he got a car, Teresa?"

"He doesn't need a car."

"How old do you think I am, Teresa?"

"How do I know how old you are?"

"Oh, go ahead, guess."

"Why should I guess how old you are?"

"Oh, go ahead, Teresa."

"Eighty."

"Teresa!"

With that little baby face she had, though, she really looked younger than she was (younger than Teresa, in fact), and she knew it. But then she never did a lick of work in her life—but how could she, the poor thing!

Dolly had one very bad habit. They might be talking about the leopards when, suddenly, sitting perfectly still in her wheel chair, she'd catch Teresa's eye. Then, giggling slightly, she would push up her wig, inch by inch, showing more and more scalp. When this started now, Teresa looked the other way and left the room. The first time it happened, however, she'd seen all of Dolly's bone-white head. Teresa didn't know what this meant—Dolly didn't call it anything and Teresa wouldn't ask—but it certainly wasn't very nice. She thought of reporting it to Dolly's sister, but did not, each time hoping it wouldn't happen again.

But finally she did call Mrs. Shepherd and say she didn't know how much longer she could stay on the job. She really felt sorry for the poor thing, but she had to think of herself

too. Mrs. Shepherd asked Teresa to give it another chance—
at least until something turned up in her line, which might
be any day now—and Teresa said, "Well, all right . . ."

For a week they were engaged in preparations for the
priest, who had finally accepted Dolly's invitation to dinner—
for Saturday, however—and Teresa knew he intended to eat
and run, pleading confessions to be heard, and she certainly
didn't blame him. She had been asked to work Saturday and
to stay overnight because, as Dolly put it, "it might be late
before it's all over." She planned to serve ginger ale later on,
after she read her poems to him. (Dolly gave Teresa a copy
of every one she wrote, and on some days she wrote many.
Teresa kept only one, because it was a little like *Trees*.

> *A sight more lovely and sweet*
> *Nowhere on earth have I seen*
> *Than the little bundles of meat*
> *In mothers' arms I mean.*)

Teresa cleaned the whole house, and Dolly got out the
sick-call kit and checked over the candles, crucifix and cotton.
Teresa asked what she was doing—getting ready to be sick
while she had the priest in the house to pray over her? Dolly
said she knew what she was doing. She said the priest might
want to inspect the kit.

"Teresa, what dress are you going to wear tomorrow night?"

"I don't know."

"Teresa, why don't you wear your nice blue one with the
white collar and cuffs?"

"You can't fool me, Dolly. I know you. You want me to
look like the maid."

Dolly smiled and said, "Well?"

More than just put out, really hurt, Teresa retired to the

other side of the house, taking the vacuum cleaner with her. Dolly was afraid of the vacuum cleaner, and the rest of the morning Teresa kept it going strong. Often, if she craved a little peace and quiet, she would switch it on in another room and just let it run while she read a magazine. And sometimes when Dolly came snooping, Teresa got up and started after her with the vacuum cleaner, sending her wheeling and squealing back to her radio.

That day, while Dolly was in the bathtub, Teresa phoned Mrs. Shepherd. She'd had enough, she said, and was quitting at the end of the day. It was Friday, and Dolly's sister would be home over Saturday and Sunday, and maybe by Monday they'd have somebody else. Anyway, she was through. No, she wasn't mad. She was just through. She couldn't be mad at the poor thing, though that one could be very mean. Mrs. Shepherd, who must have sensed it was no use, said she understood, said she was grateful to Teresa, and would just have to buckle down and find somebody else. She thought something in light sewing would turn up very soon. In fact, she had a lead.

Teresa returned to Dolly thinking—and what if they can't find anybody to look after the poor thing?—and feeling sorry for her, until she said, "Next fall, Teresa, with winter coming on and everything, people will be looking for work. You're lucky to be here, Teresa."

"Huh! I don't have to work. I own property in Florida." Teresa's property, which she'd never seen, had cost fourteen hundred dollars in 1928, and she'd always told Dolly what they'd told her, that it would be worth a lot more someday. Recently it had been appraised at "Twenty-five dollars or maybe fifty."

When Dolly's sister came home, Teresa gave her the bad news. She was sorry, she said, going at once for her coat and things. Maybe they'd be able to get somebody by Monday.

Dolly cried. Dolly's sister, paying up only when Teresa had
her coat on, offered her an extra dollar as a bonus, but Teresa
said, "No, thanks," and hoped they understood. A dollar!

That evening Teresa celebrated by eating in a new cafeteria,
and after dinner she saw a double feature. The next day,
Saturday, she slept late. Toward sundown she thought of
Dolly: now she's dusting the furniture from her wheel chair,
now she's got the wig in her hands, tying the flower into it,
now she's waiting by the door for the priest to come, now
they're sitting down to it, now they're eating the cake Teresa
had baked, and now, much too soon for the poor thing, before
she could read her poems, the priest had gone, and the un-
opened bottle of ginger ale chilled on in the refrigerator.

By Sunday afternoon Teresa was getting tired of her little
apartment and beginning to consider a quick visit to her relatives downstate. But that evening Mrs. Shepherd called.

"Teresa?"

"Yes."

"Remember that lead I spoke to you about?"

"Yes."

"I'm afraid it fell through."

"Oh." Teresa was afraid of what was coming.

"Teresa, will you help me out—try it just one more week,
maybe just a day or two, just until I get someone?"

"Oh, no . . ."

"You won't reconsider?"

"Oh, no . . ."

"Teresa, I already told them you'd come tomorrow. I mean
I was sure you'd help me out of this spot. I mean I just knew
you'd do it for me."

"But, Mrs. Shepherd . . ."

"As a friend, Teresa?"

Teresa was holding her breath for fear she'd weaken.

"Good night, Teresa, and thanks anyway."

A few minutes later Mrs. Shepherd called again.

"I told them you weren't coming, Teresa," said Mrs. Shepherd as though she expected to be thanked for it. "Teresa, that Dolly—did you ever notice anything about her?"

"What about her? She's been an invalid all her life."

"I mean—did she seem all right—otherwise?"

"Well, I wouldn't say she's crazy—if that's what you mean."

"Then I don't understand it. She said you stole some money from her and that's why you quit. She says that's why you won't come back . . ."

Teresa lay awake until shortly before the alarm went off in the morning. At the usual time, she got on the streetcar and rode out into the suburbs. Coming up the walk, she saw Dolly's face at the level of the window sill, waiting. As always, the door chain, protection against burglars and rapists, was on, but after a moment, Dolly admitted her. "You poor thing!" Dolly cried.

Before Teresa could say a word, Dolly put the blame on herself. Having the priest over, she said, had upset her so. The money had not been stolen. She had just forgotten all about paying out for the bottle of ginger ale. "And it's still there, Teresa, untouched. Oh, let's have a glass! Let's do! In honor of your coming back!" Dolly twirled herself down the hall, calling back, "You'll have to get it down, Teresa. After all, you're the one put it 'way up there by the ice cubes." Then in a gay reproving voice, "Teresa, this wouldn't have happened if you hadn't done *that!*"

THE DEVIL WAS THE JOKER

Mr. McMaster, a hernia case convalescing in one of the four-bed wards, was fat and fifty or so, with a candy-pink face, sparse orange hair, and popeyes. ("Eyes don't permit me to read much," he had told Myles Flynn, the night orderly, more than once.) On his last evening in the hospital, as he lay in his bed smoking, his hands clasped over a box of Havanas that rested on the soft dais of his stomach, he called Myles to his bedside. He wanted to thank him, he said, and, incidentally, he had no use for "that other son of a bitch"— meaning the other orderly, an engineering student, who had prepped him for surgery. "A hell of a fine engineer he'll make. You, though, you're different—more like a doctor than an orderly—and I was surprised to hear from one of the Sisters today that you're not going into the medical field." Mr. Mc-Master said he supposed there must be other reasons for working in a hospital, but he didn't sound as though he knew any.

Myles said he'd been four years in a seminary, studying for the priesthood—until "something happened." There he stopped.

Mr. McMaster grinned. "To make a long story short," he said.

61

Myles shook his head. He'd told Mr. McMaster all there was for him to tell—all he knew. He'd simply been asked to leave, he said, and since that day, three months before, he'd just been trying to make himself useful to society, here in the hospital. Mr. McMaster suddenly got serious. He wondered, in a whisper, whether Myles was "a cradle Catholic," as if that had something to do with his expulsion, and Myles said, "Yes. Almost have to be with a name like mine." "Not a-tall," said Mr. McMaster. "That's the hell of it. The other day I met a Jew by the name of Buckingham. Some Buckingham!"

Scenting liquor on the patient's breath, Myles supposed that Mr. McMaster, like so many salesmen or executives on their last evening, wanted to get a good night's rest, to be ready for the morrow, when he would ride away in a taxicab to the daily battle of Chicago.

Again Mr. McMaster asked if Myles was a cradle Catholic, and when Myles again told him he was, Mr. McMaster said, "Call me Mac," and had Myles move the screen over to his bed. When they were hidden from the others in the ward, Mac whispered, "We don't know who they may be, whatever they say." Then he asked Myles if he'd ever heard of the Clementine Fathers. Myles had. "I'm with them," Mac said. "In a good-will capacity." He described the nature of his work, which was meeting the public, lay and clerical (the emphasis was on the latter), and "building good will" for the Clementine order and finding more readers for the *Clementine*, the family-type magazine published by the Fathers.

Myles listened patiently because he considered it part of his job to do so, but the most he could say for the magazine was that it was probably good—of its kind. Yes, he'd heard the Fathers' radio program. The program, "Father Clem Answers Your Question," was aimed at non-Catholics but it had many faithful listeners among the nuns at the hospital. And the pamphlets put out by the Fathers, many of them written by Father Clem—Myles knew them well. In the hospital waiting rooms, they were read, wrung, and gnawed upon by their captive audience. "Is Father Clem a real person?" Myles asked. "Yes, and no," Mac said, which struck Myles as descriptive of the characters created by Father Clem, an author who tackled life's problems through numberless Joans, Jeans, Bobs, and Bills, clear-thinking college kids who, coached from the wings by jolly nuns and priests, invariably got the best of the arguments they had with the poor devils they were always meeting—atheists, euthanasianists, and the like. "Drive a car?" Mac asked. Myles said yes.

Mac then said he wanted it understood he wasn't making Myles any promises, but he thought there might be a job opening up with the Fathers soon, a job such as his own. "Think it over," Mac said, and Myles did—needing only a moment. He thought of his correspondence with the hierarchy, of the nice replies, all offering him nothing. For his purposes, the job with the Fathers, unsuited as he was to it, could be ideal. Traveling around from diocese to diocese, meeting pastors and even bishops face to face in the regular course of the work, he might make the vital connection that would lead him, somehow, to the priesthood. Without a bishop he'd never get into another seminary—a bishop was more necessary than a vocation—but Myles had more than meeting the right bishop to worry about. He had lost his clerical status, and was now 1-A in the draft. The call-up might come any day.

Working with Mac would be action of a positive sort, better than continuing his fruitless correspondence, better than following such advice as he'd had from acquaintances—or even from the confessional, where, too hopefully, he'd taken his problems. There he had been told to go into business or science and get ahead, or into government and make a success

of *that,* after which, presumably, he could come—tottering—
before the bishops of the land as a man of proved ability
and, what was more important, a man of stability. When the
wise old confessor realized, however, that Myles not only had
been cast aside by the Church but was likely to be wanted
soon by the State, there had been no problem at all. His counsel had flowed swift and sure: "Enlist! Don't wait to be
drafted!"

"Don't think of it as just a job," Mac said now. "Try to think
of it as the Fathers do, and as I hope I do. Think of it as the
Work."

Myles, thinking of it as a steppingstone to ordination, said
he'd like to be considered for the job.

Mac said that of course the Fathers would have the last
say, but his word would carry some weight with them, since
Myles, if accepted, would be working under him—at first,
anyway. He then asked Myles to bring a glass of ice water,
and easy on the water. Myles, returning with a glass of ice,
noted a bottle in bed with Mac, tucked under the sheet at his
side like a nursing infant. He left them together, behind the
screen.

Two days later Myles was summoned by telegram to an
address in the Loop. He found the place, all right—an old
building with grillwork elevators affording passengers a view
of the cables. Mac was waiting for Myles at the cigar stand
downstairs. As they rode up to the Fathers' floor, he advised
Myles to forget all about his past as a seminarian, reasoning
that if this was mentioned to the Fathers, it might make a
bad impression. Myles had to agree with that, if reluctantly.

At the fifth floor, which the Fathers shared with a number
of tailors, publishers, and distributors of barbers' supplies, Mac
hustled Myles into the washroom. Myles' black overcoat, suit,

and tie were all wrong, Mac said. He told Myles to take off his coat and then he suggested that they switch ties. This they did, morosely. Mac's suit, a double-breasted Glen plaid with a precipitous drape and trousers that billowed about his disproportionately thin legs, would "just carry" the black tie, he said, and presumably his tie, with its spheres, coils, and triangles suggesting the spirit of Science and Industry, would carry Myles' black suit. "Don't want 'em to think they're hiring a creep," Mac said.

There was no trouble at all with the Fathers. Mac evidently stood high with them. He told them that Myles had gone to the University of Illinois for a time, which was news to Myles. He let it pass, though, because he remembered a conversation at the hospital during which, assuming Illinois to be Mac's old school, he had said that he'd once attended a football game at Illinois—or almost had. He had been dragooned into joining the Boy Scouts, Myles had explained, and had marched with his troop to the stadium for the season opener, admission free to Scouts, but on reaching the gates, he had remained outside, in a delayed protest against the Scouts and all their pomps. He had spent the afternoon walking under the campus elms. "Then you were there," Mac had said, which Myles had taken to mean that Mac felt as he did about those beautiful old trees.

Mac delivered a little pep talk, chiefly for the benefit of the three Fathers in the office, Myles suspected, although the words were spoken to him. He could think of nothing to say. He was more impressed by the charitable than the catechetical aspects of the Fathers' work. And yet, little as he might value their radio program, their pamphlets, their dim magazine, it would be work with which he could associate himself with some enthusiasm. It would suit his purposes far better than going into business or staying on at the hospital.

"The Work is one hundred per cent apostolic," said one of the Fathers.

Myles remembered that the Fathers ran several institutions for juvenile delinquents. "I know something of your trade schools," he said quickly.

"Would that we had more of them," said the Father sitting behind the desk. He had bloodied his face and neck in shaving. "You have to move with the times." He seemed to be the boss. On the wall behind him hung a metal crucifix, which could have come off a coffin, and a broken airplane propeller, which must have dated from the First World War. "How do you stand in the draft?" he asked Myles.

"All clear," said Mac, answering for him. Myles let that pass, too. He could tell Mac the facts later.

When Myles heard what the salary would be, he was glad he had other reasons for taking the job. The money would be the least important part of it, Mac put in, and Myles could see what he meant. But Myles didn't care about the money; he'd live on bread and water—and pamphlets. The salary made him feel better about not telling Mac and the Fathers that he intended to use his new position, if he could, to meet a bishop. The expense allowance, too, impressed him as decidedly prewar. Mac, however, seemed to be hinting not at its meanness but at Myles' possible profligacy when, in front of two more Fathers, who had come in to meet Myles, he said, "You'll have to watch your expenses, Flynn. Can't have you asking for reimbursements, you understand." As Myles was leaving, one of the new arrivals whispered to him, "I was on the road myself for a bit and I'd dearly love to go out again. Mr. Mc-Master, he's a grand companion. You'll make a great team."

Three days later the team was heading north in Mac's car, a lightweight black Cadillac, a '41—a good year for a Cadillac,

Mac said, and the right car for the job: impressive but not showy, and old enough not to antagonize people.

Myles was not sorry to be leaving Chicago. The nuns and nurses at the hospital had been happy to see him go—happy, they said, that he'd found a better job. This showed Myles how little they had ever understood him and his reasons for being at the hospital; he'd known all along that they had very little sense of vocation.

Speaking of the nurses, Myles told Mac that the corporal works of mercy had lost all meaning in the modern world, to which Mac replied that he wouldn't touch nursing with a ten-foot pole. Nursing might be a fine career for a girl, he allowed, and added, "A lot of 'em marry above themselves—marry money."

They were like two men in a mine, working at different levels, in different veins, and lost to each other. Mac, who apparently still thought of Myles as a doctor, wanted to know how much the internes and nurses knocked down and what their private lives were like—said he'd heard a few stories. When Myles professed ignorance, Mac seemed to think he was being secretive, as if the question went against the Hippocratic oath. He tried to discuss medicine, with special reference to his diet, but failed to interest Myles. He asked what the hospital did with the stiffs, and received no pertinent information, because the question happened to remind Myles of the medieval burial confraternities and he sailed into a long discussion of their blessed work, advocating its revival in the modern world.

"All free, huh?" Mac commented. "The undertakers would love that!"

Myles strove in vain for understanding, always against the wind. Mac had got the idea that Myles, in praising the burial fraternities, was advocating a form of socialized medicine, and he held on to it. "Use logic," he said. "What's right for the undertakers is right for the doctors."

They rode in silence for a while. Then Mac said, "What you say about the nurses may be true, but you gotta remember they don't have it easy." He knew how Myles felt about hospital work, he said, but instead of letting it prey on his mind, Myles should think of other things—of the better days ahead. Mac implied that Myles' talk about the corporal works was just a cover-up for his failure to get into anything better.

Myles restated his position. Mac, with noticeable patience, said that Myles was too hard on people—too critical of the modern world. "Give it time," he said. When Myles persisted, Mac said, "Let's give it a rest, huh? You wanna take it awhile?" He stopped the car and turned the wheel over to Myles. After watching him pass a Greyhound bus, he appeared to be satisfied that the car was in good hands, and went to sleep.

The first night on the road they stopped in a small town, at the only hotel, which had no bar, and Mac suggested that they go out for a drink. In a tavern, the bartender, when he found out they were from Chicago, showed them his collection of matchbooks with nudes on the cover.

"I have a friend that'll get you all that you want," Mac said to him. "You better avert your eyes, son," he said to Myles. "This is some of that modern world you don't like. He doesn't like our modern world," Mac said to the bartender.

"Maybe he don't know what he's missing."

The bartender seemed anxious to make a deal until Mac asked him to put down a little deposit "as evidence of good faith."

"Do I have to?"

"To me it's immaterial," Mac said. "But I notice it sometimes speeds delivery."

"I can wait."

"All right, if you're sure you can. You write your name and address on a slip of paper and how many you want." While the bartender was doing this, Mac called over to him, "Don't forget your zone number."

"We don't have 'em in this town."

"Oh," Mac said. He gave Myles a look, the wise, doped look of a camel.

The bartender brought the slip of paper over to Mac. "They gotta be as good as them I got—or better," he said, and walked away.

Mac, watching him, matched him word for step: "When-you-gonna-get-those-corners-sawed-off-your-head?"

Leaving the tavern with Mac, Myles saw the wind take the slip of paper up the street.

"My friend can do without that kind of business," Mac said.

Mac began operations on a freezing cold day in central Wisconsin, and right away Myles was denied his first opportunity. While Mac went into a chancery office to negotiate with the bishop, who would (or would not) grant permission to canvass the diocese, Myles had to wait outside in the car, with the engine running; Mac said he was worried about the battery. This bishop was one with whom Myles had already corresponded unsuccessfully, but that was small consolation to him, in view of his plan to plead his case before as many bishops as possible, without reference to past failures. How he'd manage it with Mac in attendance, he didn't know. Perhaps he could use the initial interview for analysis only and, attempting to see the bishop as an opponent in a game, try to uncover his weakness, and then call back alone later and play upon it. Myles disapproved of cunning, and rather doubted whether he could carry out such a scheme. But he also recalled that puzzling but practical advice, "Be ye therefore wise as serpents

and simple as doves," the first part of which the bishops themselves, he believed, were at such pains to follow in their deal-
ings with him.

The next day Mac invited Myles to accompany him indoors
when he paid his calls upon the pastors. The day was no
warmer but Mac said nothing about the battery. He said,
"You've got a lot to learn, son," and proceeded to give Myles
some pointers. In some dioceses, according to Mac, the bishop's permission was all you needed; get that, and the pastors—
always excepting a few incorrigibles—would drop like ripe
fruit. Unfortunately, in such dioceses the bishop's permission
wasn't always easy to obtain. Of course you got in to see
bishops personally (this in reply to a question from Myles),
but most of the time you were working with pastors. There
were two kinds of pastors, Mac said—those who honestly believed they knew everything and those who didn't. With the
first, it was best to appear helpless (as, in fact, you were) and
try to get them interested in doing your job for you. With
the other kind, you had to appear confident, promise them
the moon—something they were always looking for anyway—
tell them a change might come over their people if they were
exposed to the pamphlets and the *Clementine*. Of course,
no pastor had a right to expect such a miracle, but many did
expect it even so, if the pamphlets and the *Clementine* hadn't
been tried in the parish before. You'd meet some, though, Mac
said, who would be cold, even opposed, to the Work, and
offensive to you, and with them you took a beating—but cheerfully, hoping for a change of heart later. More than one of
that kind had come around in the end, he said, and one of
them had even written a glowing letter to the Fathers, compli-
menting them on the high type of layman they had working
for them, and had placed an order for a rack of pamphlets
on condition that Mac received credit for it. Then there were

the others—those who would do everything they could to help you, wanted to feed you and put you up overnight, but they, for some reason, were found more often in the country, or in poor city parishes, where little could be accomplished and where you seldom went.

On the third day out, they came across one of the incorrigibles. He greeted them with a snarl. "You guys're a breed apart," he said. Myles was offended, but Mac, undaunted, went into his routine for cracking hard nuts. "Don't know much about this job, I'm ashamed to say," he said, "but it's sure a lot of fun learning." The pastor, instead of going out of his way to help a cheerful soul like Mac (and a nervous one like Myles), ordered them out of the rectory, produced a golf club when they didn't go and, when they did, stood at the front window, behind a lace curtain, until they drove off.

Before the end of the first week, Myles discovered that Mac wasn't really interested in getting permission to canvass a parish house-to-house. He said he just didn't care that much about people. What he liked was co-operation; he liked to have a pastor in the pulpit doing the donkey work and the ushers in the aisles dispensing pencil stubs and subscription blanks, with him just sitting at a card table in the vestibule after Mass, smiling at the new subscribers as they passed out, making change, and croaking, "God love you." That was what Mac called "a production." He operated on a sliding scale— a slippery one, Myles thought. In a big, well-to-do parish, where the take would be high, Mac cut prices. He was also prepared to make an offering toward the upkeep of the church, or to the pastor's favorite charity (the latter was often the former), and to signify his intention beforehand. He had to hustle, he said, in order to meet the stiff competition of the missionaries; a layman, even if he represented a recognized religious order, was always at a disadvantage. Fortunately, he said, there were quite a few secular pastors who, though they didn't care for the orders, didn't consider the struggling Clementines a menace. But there weren't many pastors with flourishing parishes who would co-operate with Mac or with anybody. They were sitting pretty, Mac said, and they knew it. If he now and then succeeded with one of them, it was only because he was liked personally—or, as it seemed to Myles, because of what Mac called "the package deal." The package deal didn't actually involve the Work, Mac was careful to explain, but it sometimes helped it. And, Myles felt, compromised it.

The package deal always began with Mac's opening his bag of tricks. It was a Gladstone bag, which he had got from a retired cooky salesman. When open, it looked like a little stadium, and where the cookies had once been on display, in their individual plastic sections, ranged in tiers, there were now rosaries, medals, scapulars—religious goods of the usual quality, which didn't catch the eye in many rectories. But there were also playing cards with saints as face cards—in one deck the Devil was the joker—and these were new to some priests, as they were to Myles, and had strong educational appeal. Children could familiarize themselves with the lives of the saints from them, and there were other decks, which taught Christian doctrine. Mac had a new kind of rosary, too. It was made of plastic, to fit the hand, and in function and appearance it was similar to an umpire's ball-and-strike indicator. Each time a little key was punched, the single dial, which showed the Mysteries—Sorrowful, Joyful, and Glorious— revolved a notch, and for the Ave Marias there was a modest tick, for the Pater Nosters an authoritative click. Mac had difficulty explaining the new rosary's purpose to some priests— *not* to replace the old model, the traditional beads on a string, but to facilitate prayer while driving, for the new rosary was easily attached to the steering wheel. "Of course, you still have to say the prayers," Mac would say.

Mac gave freely from his bag. Other things, however, he sold—just as an accommodation, he said, to priests, whose work naturally left them little time for shopping. He seemed to have a friend in every business that a parish priest might have to deal with. Myles saw him take large orders for automatic bingo cards (with built-in simulated corn counters), and the trunk of the car was full of catalogues and of refills for the grab bag. "There's one for you, Father," he'd say, presenting a pastor with one of the new rosaries. Later, speaking earnestly of power lawnmowers, of which he happened to have a prospectus showing pictures and prices, he'd say, "That's practically cost minus, Father. He"—referring to a friend—"can't do better than that, I know."

One day, when they were driving along, Myles, at the wheel, asked about Mac's friends.

"Friends? Who said I had any?" Mac snapped.

"I keep hearing you talking about your friends."

"Is that *so?*" Some miles later, after complete silence, Mac said, "I'm a man of many friends—and I don't make a dime on any of 'em." Still later, "The Fathers know all about it."

This Myles doubted. The Fathers were forbidden to engage in business for profit, he knew, and he believed that Mac, as their representative, was probably subject to the same prohibition. It was a question, though, whether Mac was primarily the Fathers' representative or his friends' or his own. It was hard to believe that *everyone* was only breaking even. And Myles felt sure that if the Fathers knew about the package deal, they'd think they had to act. But a replacement for Mac would be hard to find. The *Clementine*, as Myles was discovering, was not an easy magazine to sell. The pamphlets weren't moving well, either.

Without knowing it at the time, Myles saw a variation of the package deal worked on a pastor who met them in his front yard, baying, "I know all about you! Go!" Myles was more than ready to go, but Mac said, "You know, Monsignor, I believe you do know about me." "Don't call me Monsignor!" "My mistake, Father." Mac's voice was as oil being poured out. "Father, something you said just now makes me want to say something to you, only it's not anything I care to say in front of others." "Whatever you have to say can be said now," the pastor mumbled. "Believe me, Father, I can't say it—not in front of this boy," Mac said, nodding at Myles. Then, in a stage whisper to Myles, "You better go, son." Myles hesitated, expecting to hear the pastor overrule Mac, but nothing of the sort happened, and Myles went out and sat in the car. Mac and the pastor, a fierce-looking, beak-nosed Irish type, began to walk slowly around the yard, and presently disappeared behind the rectory. Then, after a bit, there was Mac, coming out the front door and calling to Myles from the porch, "Come on in!" Myles went in and shook hands with the pastor, actually a gentle silver-haired man. He asked them to stay for lunch, but Mac graciously refused, insisting it would be too much trouble for the housekeeper. On the following Sunday morning, this same pastor, a marvelous speaker, preached in behalf of the Work, calling the *Clementine* "that dandy little magazine" at all five Masses. Myles attended them all, while Mac hobnobbed with the ushers in the vestibule. Between Masses, the two of them, sitting at the card table, worked like bookmakers between races. Afterward, when they were driving away, Mac announced that the team had had its most successful day. That evening, in a new town, relaxing in the cocktail lounge of their hotel, Mac gave up his secret. He said he had diagnosed the pastor perfectly and had taken the pledge from him—that was all. Seeing that Myles disapproved, he said, "It so happened I needed it." Myles, who was getting to know Mac, couldn't quarrel with that.

Mac and Myles moved constantly from town to town and diocese to diocese, and almost every night Myles had the problem of locating suitable accommodations. He soon saw that he would not be able to afford the hotels and meals to which Mac was accustomed, and finally he complained. Mac looked hurt. He said, "We don't do the Work for profit, you know." He only got by himself, he said, by attributing part of his living expenses to the car. He wasn't misusing the swindle sheet, though; he was adapting it to circumstances beyond his control. There really *were* expenses. "I don't have to tell you that," he said. "The Fathers, God love 'em, just don't understand how prices have gone up." Myles' predecessor, a fellow named Jack, had put up in "the more reasonable hotels and rooming houses," and Mac suggested that Myles do the same, for a while. "Later, when you're doing better, you could stay in regular hotels."

"Is that what Jack did—later?" Myles asked.

"No. Jack seemed to like the kind of places he stayed in." Jack, in fact, had quit the Work in order to stay on in one of them, and was now engaged to the landlady. "In some ways, Jack wasn't meant for the Work," Mac added. "But we had some fine times together and I hated to see him go. He was a damn fine driver. Not that that's everything."

It had become an important part of Myles' job to do all the driving and put the car away at night and bring it around to the hotel in the morning for Mac and his luggage. More and more, Mac rode in the back seat. (He said he preferred the ashtray there.) But there was no glass between the front and back seats, and the arrangement did not interfere with conversation or alter Mac's friendliness. Occasionally, they'd arrive in a town late at night—too late for Myles to look for one of the more reasonable places—and Mac would say, mercifully, "Come on. Stay with me." And on those nights Mac would pick up the tab. This could also happen even when they arrived in plenty of time for Myles to look around, provided the drive had been a long one and Myles had played the good listener.

The association between the two was generally close, and becoming closer. Mac talked frankly about his ex-friends, of whom there were many—mostly former associates or rivals in the general-merchandise field, double-crossers to a man. The first few times this happened, Myles controlled his desire to tell Mac that by damning others, as he did, he damned the whole human race—damned himself, in fact. One day, after Mac had finished with his old friends and with his wife (who was no good), and was beginning to go to work on the Jews (who also had given him nothing but trouble), Myles did tell him. He presented an idea he held to be even greater than the idea of brotherhood. It was the doctrine of the Mystical Body of Christ. Humanity was one great body, Myles explained, all united with Christ, the Saviour. Mac acted as though the doctrine were a new one on him. "One great body, huh? Sounds like the Mystical Knights of the Sea," he said, and talked for a while of Amos and Andy and of the old days when they'd been Sam and Henry. That was the afternoon that Mac got onto the subject of his dream.

Mac's dream—as he spoke, the snow was going from gray to ghostly blue and the lights were coming on in the houses along the way—was to own a turkey ranch and a church-goods store. What he really wanted was the ranch, he said, but he supposed he'd have to play it safe and have the store, too. Turkeys could be risky. With the general revival of interest in religion, however, a well-run church-goods store would be sure to succeed. He'd sell by mail, retail and wholesale, and there'd be discounts for everybody—not just for the clergy, though, of course, he'd have to give them the usual break. The store would be a regular clearinghouse: everything from holy cards to statues—products of all the leading manufacturers.

"Sort of a supermarket?" Myles asked, thinking of chalices and turkeys roosting all in a row.

"That's the idea."

"It'd be nice if there were one place in this country where you could get an honest piece of ecclesiastical art," Myles said.

"I'd have that, too, later," Mac said. "A custom department."

They were getting along very well, different as they were. Mac *was* a good traveling companion, ready wherever they went with a little quick information about the towns ("Good for business," "All Swedes," "Wide open"), the small change of real knowledge.

One day, when they were passing through Superior, Wisconsin, Mac said that originally the iron-ore interests had planned to develop the town. Property values had been jacked up, however, by operators too smart for their own good, and everything had gone to Duluth, with its relatively inferior harbor. That was how Superior, favored by nature, had become what it was, a small town with the layout of a metropolis.

"It's easier to move mountains than greedy hearts," Myles commented.

"I wouldn't know," Mac said.

Myles found the story of Superior instructive—positively Biblical, he said. Another case of man's greed. The country thereabouts also proved interesting to Myles, but difficult for

Mac when Myles began to expound on the fished-out lakes (man's greed), the cut-over timberland (man's greed), the poor Indians (the *white* man's greed). The high-grade ore pits, Mac foolishly told him, were almost exhausted.

"Exhausted for what?" Myles asked.

"Steel," said Mac, who didn't realize the question had been rhetorical.

"This car!" said Myles, with great contempt. "War!" Looking into the rearview mirror, he saw Mac indulging in what was becoming a habit with him—pulling on his ear lobes.

"What *are* you?" Mac finally demanded. "Some kind of a new damn fool?"

But Myles never gave up on him. He went right on making his points, laying the ground for an awakening; it might never come to Mac, but Myles carried on as if it might at any moment. Mac, allied with the modern world for better or worse, defended the indefensible and fought back. And when logic failed him, he spluttered, "You talk like you got holes in your head," or, "Quit moanin'!" or, "Who you think you are, buster—the Pope?"

"This is when you're *really* hard to take!" Mac said one day, when the news from Korea was bad and Myles was most telling. Myles continued obliviously, perceiving moral links between Hiroshima and Korea and worse things to come, and predicting universal retribution, weeping, and gnashing of teeth. "And why?" he said. "Greed!"

"Greed! Greed! Is that all you can think about? No wonder they had to get rid of you!"

A few miles of silence followed, and then a few well-chosen words from Mac, who had most certainly been thinking, which was just what Myles was always trying to get him to do. "Are you sure the place you escaped from was a seminary?" he asked.

But Myles let him see he could take even this, turning the other cheek so gracefully that Mac could never know his words were touching a sore spot.

Later that day, in the middle of a sermon from Myles, they passed a paddy wagon and Mac said, "They're looking for you." Ever after, if Myles discoursed too long or too well on the state of the modern world, there came a tired but amiable croaking from the back seat, "They're looking for you."

At night, however, after the bars closed, it was *Mac* who was looking for Myles. If they were staying at the same hotel, he'd knock at Myles' door and say, "Care to come over to the room for a drink?" At first, Myles, seeing no way out of it, would go along, though not for a drink. He drank beer when he drank, or wine, and there was never any of either in Mac's room. It was no fun spending the last hour of the day with Mac. He had a lot of stories, but Myles often missed the point of them, and he knew none himself—none that Mac would appreciate, anyway. What Cardinal Merry del Val had said to Cardinal Somebody Else—the usual seminary stuff. But Mac found a subject to interest *him*. He began denying that Myles was a cradle Catholic. Myles, who had never seen in this accident of birth the personal achievement that Mac seemed to see, would counter, "All right. What if I weren't one?"

"You see? You see?" Mac would say, looking very wise and drunk. Then, as if craving and expecting a confession, he'd say, "You can tell *me*."

Myles had nothing to tell, and Mac would start over again, on another tack. Developing his thought about what he called Myles' "ideas," he would arrive at the only possible conclusion: Myles wasn't a Catholic at all. He was probably only a smart-aleck convert who had come into the Church when the coming was good, and only *thought* he was in.

"Do you deny the possibility of conversion?" Myles would ask, though there was small pleasure in theologizing with someone like Mac.

Mac never answered the question. He'd just keep saying, "You call yourself a *Catholic*—a *cradle* Catholic?"

The first time Myles said no to Mac's invitation to come over and have one, it worked. The next time, Mac went back to his room only to return with his bottle, saying, "Thought you might like to have one in your pajamas." That was the night Myles told Mac, hopefully, that whiskey was a Protestant invention; in Ireland, for example, it had been used, more effectively than the penal laws, to enslave the faithful. "Who're you kiddin'!" Mac wailed.

Mere admonishment failed with Mac. One day, as they were driving through primitive country, Myles delivered a regular sermon on the subject of drink. He said a man possessed by drink was a man possessed by the Devil. He said that Mac, at night, was very like a devil, going about hotel corridors "as a roaring lion goeth about seeking whom he may devour." This must have hit Mac pretty hard, for he said nothing in his own defense; in fact, he took it very well, gazing out at the pine trees, which Myles, in the course of his sermon, had asked him to consider in all their natural beauty. That afternoon, they met another hard nut—and Mac took the pledge again, which closed the deal for a production on the following Sunday, and also, he seemed to think, put him into Myles' good graces. "I wish I could find one that could give it to me and make it stick," he said.

"Don't come to me when I'm a priest," said Myles, who had still to see his first bishop.

That night Mac and the bottle were at the door again. Myles, in bed, did not respond. This was a mistake. Mac phoned the office and had them bring up a key and open

Myles' door, all because he thought Myles might be sick. "I love that boy!" he proclaimed, on his way back to his room at last. Later that night Myles heard him in the corridor, at a little distance, with another drunk. Mac was roaring, "I'm seein' who I may devour!"

More and more, Myles and Mac were staying together in the same hotels, and Myles, though saving money by this arrangement (money, however, that he never saw), wondered if he wasn't paying too much for economy. He felt slightly kept. Mac only wanted him handy late at night, it seemed, so as to have someone with whom to take his pleasure, which was haranguing. Myles now understood better why Jack had liked the places he stayed in. Or was this thing that Mac was doing to him nightly something new for Mac? Something that Myles had brought upon himself? He was someone whom people looking for trouble always seemed to find. It had happened to him in the hospital, in the seminary, in the Boy Scouts. If a million people met in one place, and he was there, he was certain that the worst of them would rise as a man and make for him.

But Mac wasn't always looking for trouble. One afternoon, for no reason at all, he bought Myles a Hawaiian sports shirt. "For next summer," Mac said, as if they would always be together. The shirt was a terrible thing to look at—soiled merchandise picked up at a sale—but it might mean something. Was it possible that Mac, in his fashion, liked him?

"A fellow like you might handle that end of it," Mac said one day in the car. He had been talking about the store part of his dream and how he would put out a big catalogue in which it would be wise for manufacturers—and maybe religious orders, too—to buy advertising if they expected to do business with him. "Interested?" he asked.

Myles was definitely not interested, but he was touched by the offer, since it showed that Mac trusted him. It was time to put matters straight between them. Myles spoke then of *his* dream—of the great desire he had to become a priest. Not a punch-drunk seminary professor or a fat cat in a million-dollar parish, he said, but a simple shepherd ministering gently to the poorest of God's poor. He wouldn't mind being a priest-worker, like those already functioning so successfully in France, according to reports reaching him. "That can't happen here," Mac said. Myles, however, saw difficult times ahead for the nation— Here Mac started to open his mouth but grabbed instead for his ears. Myles felt pretty sure that there would soon be priest-workers slaving away in fields and factories by day and tending to the spiritual needs of their poor fellow-workers by night.

"Poor?" Mac asked. "What about the unions? When I think what those boys take home!"

Myles then explored the more immediate problem of finding a bishop to sponsor him.

Mac said he knew several quite well and he might speak to them.

"I wish you would," Myles said. "The two I've seen looked impossible." Then, having said that much—too much—he confessed to Mac his real reason for taking the job: the urgency of his position with regard to Selective Service.

Immediately, Mac, who had not been paying much attention, released an ear for listening. He appeared ill-disposed toward Myles' reluctance to serve in the armed forces, or, possibly, toward such frankness.

"I can't serve two masters," Myles said. Mac was silent; he'd gone absolutely dead. "Are you a veteran?" Myles asked.

"Since you ask," Mac said, "I'll tell you. I served and was wounded—honorably—in both World Wars. If there's another one, I hope to do my part. Does that answer your question?" Myles said that it did, and he could think of nothing to say just then that wouldn't hurt Mac's feelings.

That night, Mac, in his cups, surpassed himself. He got through with the usual accusations early and began threatening Myles with "exposure." "Dodgin' the draft!" Mac howled. "I oughta turn you in."

Myles said he hadn't broken the law *yet*.

"But you *intend* to," Mac said. "I oughta turn you in."

"I'll turn myself in when the time comes," Myles said.

"Like hell you will. You'll go along until they catch up with you. Then they'll clap you in jail—where you belong."

"Maybe you're right," Myles said, thinking of St. Paul and other convicts.

"Then you'll wish you were in the Army—where you belong. I'm not sure it's not my duty to report you. Let's see your draft card."

Myles let him see it.

" 'Flynn, Myles'—that you? How do I know you're not somebody else by the same name?"

Myles made no reply. Had prohibition been so wrong, he wondered.

"Don't wanna incriminate yourself, huh? Hey, you're 1-A! Didja see that?"

Myles explained, as he had before, that he was awaiting his induction notice.

"Bet you are! Bet you can hardly wait! I'd better hold onto this." Mac slipped Myles' draft card into his pocket.

In the morning, Myles got the card back. Mac, sober, returned it, saying he'd found it in his room, where Myles (who had not been there) must have dropped it. "Better hold on to that," Mac said.

The next night Myles managed to stay in a rooming house, out of reach, but the following night they were together again, and Mac asked to see Myles' draft card again. Myles wouldn't give it up. "I deny your authority," he said, himself emboldened by drink—two beers.

"Here's my authority!" Mac cried. He loosened his trousers and pulled up his shirt in front, exposing a stomach remarkably round, smooth, veined, and, in places, blue, like a world globe. There was a scar on it. "How d'ya think I got that?"

"Appendicitis," Myles said.

There was no doubt of it. The scar testified to Mac's fraudulence as nothing else had, and for once Mac seemed to know it. He'd strayed into a field in which he believed Myles to be supreme. Putting his stomach away, he managed a tone in which there was misgiving, outrage, and sarcasm. "That's right. That's right. You know everything. You were a bedpan jockey. I forgot about that."

Myles watched him, amused. Mac might have saved himself by telling the truth or by quickly laughing it off, but he lied on. "Shrapnel—some still inside," he said. He coughed and felt his stomach, as if his lungs were there, but he didn't get it out again. "Not asking *you* to believe it," he said. "Won't show *you* my other wound."

"Please don't," said Myles. He retired that night feeling that he had the upper hand.

One week later, leaving a town in Minnesota where they had encountered a difficult bishop, Mac ordered Myles to stop at a large, gabled rectory of forbidding aspect. As it turned out, however, they enjoyed a good dinner there, and afterward the pastor summoned three of his colleagues for a little game of blackjack—in Mac's honor, Myles heard him say as the players trooped upstairs.

Myles spent the evening downstairs with the curate. While they were eating some fudge the curate had made that afternoon, they discovered that they had many of the same enthusiasms and prejudices. The curate wanted Myles to understand that the church was not his idea, loaded up, as it was, with junk. He was working on the pastor to throw out most of the statues and all the vigil lights. It was a free-talking, free-swinging session, the best evening for Myles since leaving the seminary. In a nice but rather futile tribute to Myles, the curate said that if the two of them were pastors, they might, perhaps, transform the whole diocese. He in no way indicated that he thought there was anything wrong with Myles because he had been asked to leave the seminary. He believed, as Myles did, that there was no *good* reason for the dismissal. He said he'd had trouble getting through himself and he thought that the seminary, as an institution, was probably responsible for the way Stalin, another aspirant to the priesthood, had turned out. The curate also strongly disapproved of Mac, and of Myles' reasons for continuing in the Work. He said the Clementines were a corny outfit, and no bishop in his right mind, seeing Myles with Mac, would ever take a chance on him. The curate thought that Myles might be playing it too cautious. He'd do better, perhaps, just to go around the country, hitchhiking from see to see, washing dishes if he had to, but calling on bishops personally—as many as he could in the time that remained before he got his induction notice.

"How many bishops have you actually seen?" the curate asked.

"Three. But I couldn't say anything with Mac right there. I would've gone back later, though, if there'd been a chance at all with those I saw."

The curate sniffed. "How could you tell?" he asked. "I

thought you were desperate. You just *can't* be guided entirely
by private revelation. You have a higher injunction: 'Seek, and
you shall find.' Perhaps you still haven't thought this thing
through. I wonder. Perhaps you don't pray enough?"

Myles, noticing in the curate a tendency to lecture and
feeling that he'd suffered one "perhaps" too many, defended
himself, saying, "The man we met today wouldn't let us set
foot on church property in his diocese. What can you do with
a bishop like that?"

"The very one you should have persevered with! Moses, you
may remember, had to do more than look at the rock. He had
to strike it."

"Twice, unfortunately," murmured Myles, not liking the anal-
ogy. Moses, wavering in his faith, had struck twice and had
not reached the Promised Land; he had only seen it in the
distance, and died.

"It may not be too late," the curate said. "I'd try that one
again if I were you."

Myles laughed. "*That* one was your own bishop," he said.

"The bishop said that?" The curate showed some alarm and
seemed suddenly a lot less friendly. "Is that why you're here,
then—why Mac's here, I mean?"

"I couldn't tell you why I'm here," Myles said. In Mac's defense, he said, "I don't think he's mentioned the Work here."
It was true. Mac and the pastor had hit it off right away, talking of other things.

"I heard him trying to sell the pastor a new roof—a copper
one. Also an oil burner. Does he deal in *those* things?" the
curate asked.

"He has friends who do." Myles smiled. He wanted to say
more on this subject to amuse the curate, if that was still possible; he wanted to confide in him again; he wanted to say
whatever would be necessary to save the evening. But the

shadow of the bishop had fallen upon them. There were only crumbs on the fudge plate; the evening had ended. It was bedtime, the curate said. He offered Myles a Coke, which Myles refused, then showed him to a couch in the parlor, gave him a blanket, and went off to bed.

Some time later—it was still night—Mac woke Myles and they left the rectory. Mac was sore; he said he'd lost a bundle. He climbed into the back seat and wrapped himself in the car rug. "A den of thieves. I'm pretty sure I was taken. Turn on the heater." And then he slept while Myles drove away toward the dawn.

The next day, as they were having dinner in another diocese, another town, another hotel—Mac looked fresh; he'd slept all day—Myles told him that he was quitting.

"Soon?" said Mac.

"Right away."

"Give me a little time to think about it."

After dinner, Mac drew one of his good cigars out of its aluminum scabbard. "What is it? Money? Because if it is——" Mac said, puffing on the cigar, and then, looking at the cigar and not at Myles, he outlined his plans. He'd try to get more money for Myles from the Fathers, more take-home dough and more for expenses. He'd sensed that Myles had been unhappy in some of those flea bags; Myles might have noticed that they'd been staying together oftener. Ultimately, if the two of them were still together and everything went right, there might be a junior partnership for Myles in the store. "No," Mac said, looking at Myles. "I can see that's not what you want." He turned to the cigar again and asked, "Well, why not?" He invited Myles up to his room, where, he said, he might have something to say that would be of interest to him.

Upstairs, after making himself a drink, Mac said that he just might be able to help Myles in the only way he wanted to be helped. He was on fairly good terms with a number of bishops, as Myles might have gathered, but an even better bet would be the Clementines. Myles could join the order as a lay brother—*anybody* could do that—swiftly win the confidence of his superiors, then switch to the seminary, and thus complete his studies for the priesthood. "I might be able to give you such a strong recommendation that you could go straight into the seminary," Mac said. "It would mean losing you, of course. Don't like that part. Or *would* it? What's to stop us from going on together, like now, after you get your degree?"

"After *ordination?*" Myles asked.

"There you are!" Mac exclaimed. "Just shows it's a natural—us working as a team. What I don't know, you do."

While Mac strengthened his drink just a little—he was cutting down—Myles thanked him for what he'd done to date and also for what he was prepared to do. He said that he doubted, however, that he was meant for the Clementines or for the community life, and even if he were, there would still be the problem of finding a bishop to sponsor him. "Oh, *they'd* do all that," Mac said. Myles shook his head. He was quitting. He had to intensify his efforts. He wasn't getting to see many bishops, was he? Time was of the essence. He had a few ideas he wanted to pursue on his own (meaning he had one—to have another crack at the curate's bishop). The induction notice, his real worry, might come any day.

"How d'ya know you're all right physically?" Mac asked him. "You don't look very strong to me. I took you for a born 4-F. For all you know, you might be turned down and out lookin' for a job. In the circumstances, I couldn't promise to hold this one open forever."

With the usual apprehension, Myles watched Mac pour another drink. Could Mac want so badly for an underpaid chauffeur, he wondered. Myles' driving was his only asset. As a representative of the Fathers, he was a flop, and he knew it, and so did Mac. Mac, in his own words, was the baby that delivered the goods. But no layman could be as influential as Mac claimed to be with the Fathers, hard up though they were for men and money. Mac wouldn't be able to help with any bishop in his right mind. But Mac did want him around, and Myles, who could think of no one else who did, was almost tempted to stay as long as he could. Maybe he *was* 4-F.

Later that evening Mac, still drinking, put it another way, or possibly said what he'd meant to say earlier. "Hell, you'll never pass the mental test. Never let a character like you in the Army." The Fathers, though, would be glad to have Myles, if Mac said the word.

Myles thanked him again. Mac wanted him to drive the car, to do the Work, but what he wanted still more, it was becoming clear, was to have a boon companion, and Myles knew he just couldn't stand to be it.

"You're not my type," Mac said. "You haven't got it—the velocity, I mean—but maybe that's why I like you."

Myles was alone again with his thoughts, walking the plank of his gloom.

"Don't worry," Mac said. "I'll always have a spot in my heart for you. A place in my business."

"In the supermarket?"

Mac frowned. Drinking, after a point, made him appear a little cross-eyed. "I wish you wouldn't use that word," he said distinctly. "If y'wanna know, your trouble's words. Make y'self harda take. Don't *have* to be jerk. Looka you. Young. Looka me. Dead. Not even Catholic. Bloody Orangeman. 'S truth."

Myles couldn't believe it. And then he could, almost. He'd

never seen Mac at Mass on Sundays, either coming or going, except when they were working, and then Mac kept to the vestibule. The bunk that Mac had talked about Myles' being a cradle Catholic began to make sense.

"Now you're leaving the Work, I tell you," Mac was saying. "Makes no difference now." They were in Minnesota, staying in a hotel done in the once popular Moorish style, and the ceiling light and the shades of the bed lamps, and consequently the walls and Myles' face, were dead orange and Mac's face was bloody orange.

Myles got up to leave.

"Don't go," Mac said. He emptied the bottle.

But Myles went, saying it was bedtime. He realized as he said it that he sounded like the curate the night before.

Ten minutes later Mac was knocking at Myles' door. He was in his stocking feet, but looked better, like a drunk getting a hold on himself.

"Something to read," he said. "Don't feel like sleeping."

Myles had some books in his suitcase, but he left them there. "I didn't get a paper," he said.

"Don't want that," Mac said. He saw the Gideon Bible on the night stand and went over to it. "Mind if I swipe this?"

"There's probably one in your room."

Mac didn't seem to hear. He picked up the Gideon. "The Good Book," he said.

"I've got a little Catholic Bible," Myles said. The words came out of themselves—the words of a diehard proselytizer.

"Have you? Yeah, that's the one I want."

"I can't recommend it," Myles said, on second thought. "You better take the other one, for reading. It's the King James."

"Hell with that!" Mac said. He put the King James from him.

Myles went to the suitcase and got out his portable Bible. He stood with it at the door, making Mac come for it, and then, still withholding it, led him outside into the corridor, where he finally handed it over.

"How you feel now, about that other?" Mac asked.

For a moment, Myles thought he was being asked about his induction, which Mac ordinarily referred to as "that other," and not about Mac's dark secret. When he got Mac's meaning, he said, "Don't worry about me. I won't turn you in."

In the light of his activities, Mac's not being a Catholic was in his favor, from Myles' point of view; as an honest faker Mac was more acceptable, though many would not see it that way. There was something else, though, in Mac's favor—something unique; he was somebody who liked Myles just for himself. He had been betrayed by affection—and by the bottle, of course.

Myles watched Mac going down the corridor in his stocking feet toward his room, holding the Bible and swaying just a little, as if he were walking on calm water. He wasn't so drunk.

The next morning Mac returned the Bible to Myles in his room and said, "I don't know if you realize it or not, but I'm sorry about last night. I guess I said a lot of things I shouldn't have. I won't stand in your way any longer." He reached into his pocket and took out his roll. "You'll need some of this," he said.

"No, thanks," Myles said.

"You sure?"

Myles was sure.

"Forget anything I might have said." Mac eased over to the window and looked out upon the main street. "I don't know what, but I might have said something." He came back to Myles. He was fingering his roll, holding it in both hands, a fat red squirrel with a nut. "You sure now?"

Myles said yes, he was sure, and Mac reluctantly left him.

Myles was wondering if that had been their good-by when,

a few minutes later, Mac came in again. His manner was different. "I'll put it to you like this," he said. "You don't say anything about me and I won't say anything about you. Maybe we both got trouble. You know what I'm talking about?"

Myles said that he thought he knew and that Mac needn't worry.

"They may never catch you," Mac said, and went away again. Myles wondered if *that* had been their good-by.

Presently Mac came in again. "I don't remember if I told you this last night or not. I know I was going to, but what with one thing and another last night, and getting all hung up——"

"Well?"

"Kid"—it was the first time Mac had called him that—"I'm not a Catholic."

Myles nodded.

"Then I did say something about it?"

Myles nodded again. He didn't know what Mac was trying now, only that he was trying something.

"I don't know what I am," Mac said. "My folks weren't much good. I lost 'em when I was quite young. And you know about my wife." Myles knew about her. "No damn good."

Myles listened and nodded while all those who had ever failed Mac came in for slaughter. Mac ordinarily did this dirty work in the car, and it had always seemed to Myles that they threw out the offending bodies, one by one, making room for the fresh ones. It was getting close in the room. Mac stood upright amid a wreckage of carcasses—with Myles.

"You're the only one I can turn to," he said. "I'd be afraid to admit to anyone else what I've just admitted to you—I mean to a priest. As you know, I'm pretty high up in the Work, respected, well thought of, and all that, and you can imagine

what your average priest is going to think if *I* come to him—
to be baptized!"

The scene rather appealed to Myles, but he looked grave.

"I know what you're thinking," Mac said. "Don't think I
don't know the awful risk I'm taking now, with my immortal
soul and all. Gives me a chill to think of it. But I still can't
bring myself to do the right thing. Not if it means going to
a priest. Sure to be embarrassing questions. The Fathers could
easily get wind of it back in Chicago."

Myles was beginning to see what Mac had in mind.

"As I understand it, you don't have to be a priest to baptize
people," Mac continued. "*Anybody* can do it in an emergency.
You know that, of course."

Myles, just a step ahead of him, was thinking of the pastors
who'd been deceived into giving Mac the pledge. It looked
a lot like the old package deal.

"We could go over there," Mac said, glancing at the washbowl in the corner. "Or there's my room, if it'd be more ap-
propriate." He had a bathroom.

Myles hardened. "If you're asking *me* to do it," he said, "the
answer's no." Myles was now sure that Mac had been baptized
before—perhaps many times, whenever he had need of it. "I
couldn't give you a proper certificate anyway," Myles added.
"You'd want that."

"You mean if I wanted to go on with it and come into the
Catholic Church? All the way in? Is that what you mean?"

Myles didn't mean that at all, but he said, "I suppose so."

"Then you do get me?" Mac demanded.

Myles stiffened, knowing that he was in grave danger of
being in on Mac's conversion, and feeling, a moment later,
that this—this conversion—like the pledge and baptism, must
have happened before. He hastened to say, "No. I don't get
you and I don't *want* to."

Mac stood before him, silent, with bowed head, the beaten man, the man who'd asked for bread and received a stone, who'd asked for a fish and got a serpent.

But no, Mac wasn't that at all, Myles saw. He was the serpent, the nice old serpent with Glen-plaid markings, who wasn't *very* poisonous. He'd been expecting tenderness, but he had caught the forked stick just behind the head. The serpent was quiet. Was he dead? "I give you my word that I'll never tell anybody what you've told me," Myles said. "So far as I'm concerned, you're a Catholic—a cradle Catholic if you like. I hold no grudge against you for anything you've said, drunk or sober. I hope you'll do the same for me."

"I will that," Mac said, and began to speak of their "relationship," of the inspiration Myles had been to him from the very first. There was only one person responsible for the change in his outlook, he said, and it might interest Myles to know that *he* was that person.

Myles saw that he'd let up on the stick too soon. The serpent still had plenty left. Myles pressed down on him. "I want out, Mac," he said. "I'm not a priest yet. I don't *have* to listen to this. If you want me to spill the beans to the Fathers, just keep it up."

The serpent was very quiet now. Dead?

"You do see what I mean?" Myles said.

"Yeah, now I see," Mac said. He was looking only a little hurt; the flesh above his snow-white collar was changing pinks, but he was looking much better, seemingly convinced that Myles, with an excuse to harm him, and with the power to do so, would not. Mac was having his remarkable experience after all—almost a conversion. "Had you wrong," he confessed. "Thought sure you'd squeal. Thought sure you'd be the type that would. Hope you don't mind me saying that. Because you got my respect now."

Myles could see, however, that Mac liked him less for having it. But he had Mac's respect, and it was rare, and it made the day rare.

"Until I met you, why—— Well, *you* know." Mac stopped short.

Myles, with just a look, had let him feel the stick.

"We'll leave it at that," Mac said.

"If you will, I will," said Myles. He crossed the room to the washbowl, where he began to collect his razor, his toothbrush, and the shaving lotion that Mac had given him. When he turned around with these things in his hands, he saw that Mac had gone. He'd left a small deposit of gray ash on the rug near the spot where he'd coiled and uncoiled.

Later that morning Myles, as a last service and proof of good will, went to the garage and brought Mac's car around to the hotel door, and waited there with it until Mac, smoking his second cigar of the day, appeared. Myles helped him stow his luggage and refused his offer to drive him to the railroad station, if that was where Myles wanted to go. Myles had not told Mac that he intended to hitchhike back to the last town, to confront the difficult bishop and strike the rock a second time. After shaking hands, Mac began, "If I hear of anything——" but Myles silenced him with a look, and then and there the team split up.

Mac got into the Cadillac and drove off. Watching, Myles saw the car, half a block away, bite at the curb and stop. And he saw why. Mac, getting on with the Work, was offering a lift to two men all in black, who, to judge by their actions, didn't really want one. In the end, though, the black car consumed them, and slithered out of view.

A LOSING GAME

Father Fabre, coming from the bathroom, stopped and knocked at the pastor's door—something about the door had said, Why not? No sound came from the room, but the pastor had a ghostly step and there he was, opening the door an inch, giving his new curate a glimpse of the green eyeshade he wore and of the chaos in which he dwelt. Father Fabre saw the radio in the unmade bed, the correspondence, pamphlets, the folding money, and all the rest of it—what the bishop, on an official visitation, barging into the room and then hurriedly backing out, had passed off to the attending clergy as "a little unfinished business."

"Yes? Yes?"

"How about that table you promised me?"

The pastor just looked at him.

"The one for my room, remember? Something to put my typewriter on."

"See what I can do."

The pastor had said that before. Father Fabre said, "I'm using the radiator now."

The pastor nodded, apparently granting him permission to continue using it.

Father Fabre put down the old inclination to give up. "I thought you said you'd fix me up, Father."

"See what I can do, Father."

"Now?"

"Busy now."

The pastor started to close the door, which was according to the rules of their little game, but Father Fabre didn't budge, which was not according to the rules.

"Tell you what I'll do, Father," he said. "I'll just look around in the basement and you won't have to bother. I know how busy you are." Father Fabre had a strange feeling that he was getting somewhere with the pastor. Everything he'd said so far had been right, but he had to keep it up. "Of course I'll need to know the combination." He saw the pastor buck and shudder at the idea of telling anyone the combination of the lock that preserved his treasures.

"Better go with you," the pastor said, feeling his throat.

Father Fabre nodded. This was what he'd had in mind all the time. While the pastor was inside his room looking for his collar (always a chance of meeting a parishioner on the stairs), Father Fabre relaxed and fell to congratulating himself. He had been tough and it had worked. The other thing had proved a waste of time.

After a bit, though, Father Fabre took another view of the situation, knowing as he did so that it was the right one, that the door hadn't just happened to shut after the pastor, that the man wasn't coming out. Oh, that was it. The pastor had won again. He was safe in his room again, secure in the knowledge that his curate wouldn't knock and start up the whole business again, not for a while anyway.

Father Fabre went away. Going downstairs, he told himself that though he had lost, he had extended the pastor as never before, and would get the best of him yet.

Father Fabre sensed John, the janitor, before he saw him sitting in the dark under the staircase, at one of his stations. He might be found in this rather episcopal chair, which was also a hall-tree, or on a box in the furnace room, or in the choir loft behind the organ, or in the visiting priest's confessional. There were probably other places which Father Fabre didn't know about. John moved around a lot, foxlike, killing time.

Father Fabre switched on the light. John pulled himself together and managed a smile, his glasses as always frosted over with dust so that he seemed to be watching you through basement windows.

"John, you know that lock on the door to the church basement?"

John nodded.

"It's not much of a lock. Think we can open it?"

John frowned.

"A tap on the side?"

John shook his head.

"No?"

"Sorry, Father."

"So." Father Fabre turned away.

"Will you need a hammer, Father?"

"Don't think I'll need one. Sure you won't come along?"

"Awful busy, Father." But John found time to get up and accompany Father Fabre to the iron staircase that led to the church basement. There they parted. Father Fabre snapped the light switch on the wall. He wasn't surprised when nothing happened. He left the door open for light. A half flight down, pausing, he hearkened to John's distant footsteps, rapidly climbing, and then he went winding down into the gloom. At the bottom he seated himself on a step and waited.

Soon he heard a slight noise above. Rounding the last turn,

descending into view, was the pastor. "Oh, there you are," said Father Fabre, rising.

The pastor voiced no complaint—and why should he? He'd lost a trick, but Father Fabre had taken it honorably, according to the rules, in a manner worthy of the pastor himself.

Father Fabre was up on his toes, straining to see.

The pastor was fooling with something inside the fuse box on the wall, standing up to it, his back almost a shield against Father Fabre's eyes. Overhead a bulb lit up. So that was it, thought Father Fabre, coming down to earth—and to think that he'd always blamed the wiring for the way some of the lights didn't work around the church and rectory, recommending a general checkup, prophesying death by conflagration to the pastor. Father Fabre, rising again, saw the pastor screw in another fuse where none had been before. That would be the one controlling the basement lights.

The pastor dealt next with the door, dropping into a crouch to dial the lock.

Father Fabre leaned forward like an umpire for the pitch, but saw at once that it would be impossible to lift the combination. He scraped his foot in disgust, grinding a bit of fallen plaster. The pastor's fingers tumbled together. He seemed to be listening. After a moment, he began to dial again, apparently having to start all over.

"There," he said finally. He removed the lock, threw open the door, but before he went in, he stepped over to the fuse box. The overhead light went out. Father Fabre entered the basement, where he had been only once before, and not very far inside then. The pastor secured the door behind them. From a convenient clothes tree he removed a black cap and put it on—protection against the dust? Father Fabre hadn't realized that the pastor, who now looked like a burglar in an insurance ad, cared. The pastor glanced at him. Quickly

Father Fabre looked away. He gazed around him in silence.

It was impossible to decide what it all meant. In the clothes tree alone, Father Fabre noted a cartridge belt, a canteen stenciled with the letters U.S., a pair of snowshoes, an old bicycle tire of wrinkled red rubber, a beekeeper's veil. One of Father Fabre's first services to the pastor had been to help John carry two workbenches into the basement. At that time he had thought the pastor must have plans for a school in which manual training would be taught. Now he felt that the pastor had no plans at all for any of the furniture and junk. A few of the unemployed statues when seen at a distance, those with their arms extended, appeared to be trying to get the place straightened up, carrying things, but on closer examination they, too, proved to be preoccupied with a higher kind of order, and carrying crosiers.

The pastor came away from a rack containing billiard cues, ski poles, and guns.

"Here," he said, handing an air rifle to Father Fabre.

Father Fabre accepted the gun, tipped it, listening to the BB shot bowling up and down inside. "What's this for?"

"Rats."

"Couldn't kill a rat with this, could I?"

"Could."

But Father Fabre noticed that the pastor was arming himself with a .22 rifle. "What's that?" he asked covetously.

"This gun's not accurate," said the pastor. "From a shooting gallery."

"What's wrong with trapping 'em?"

"Too smart."

"How about poison?"

"Die in the walls."

The pastor moved off, bearing his gun in the way that was supposed to assure safety.

Father Fabre held his gun the same way and followed the pastor. He could feel the debris closing in, growing up behind him. The path ahead appeared clear only when he looked to either side. He trailed a finger in the dust on a table top, revealing the grain. He stopped. The wood was maple, he thought, maple oiled and aged to the color of saddle leather. There were little niches designed to hold glasses. The table was round, a whist table, it might be, and apparently sound. Here was a noble piece of furniture that would do wonders for his room. It could be used for his purposes, and more. That might be the trouble with it. The pastor was strong for temperance. It might not be enough for Father Fabre to deplore the little niches.

"Oh, Father."

The pastor retraced his steps.

"This might do," Father Fabre said grudgingly, careful not to betray a real desire. There was an awful glazed green urn thing in the middle of the table which Father Fabre feared would leave scratches or a ring. A thing like that, which might have spent its best days in a hotel, by the elevators, belonged on the floor. Father Fabre wanted to remove it from the table, but he controlled himself.

"Don't move," said the pastor. "Spider."

Father Fabre held still while the pastor brushed it off his back. "Thanks." Father Fabre relaxed and gazed upon the table again. He had to have it. He would have it.

But the pastor was moving on.

Father Fabre followed in his steps, having decided to say nothing just then, needing more time to think. The important thing was not to seem eager. "It isn't always what we want that's best for us," the pastor had said more than once. He loved to speak of Phil Mooney—a classmate of Father Fabre's —who had been offered a year of free study at a major secular university, but who had been refused permission by the bishop. Young Mooney, as the pastor said, had taken it so well . . . "This—how about this?" said Father Fabre. He had stopped before a nightstand, a little tall for typing. "I could saw the legs off some."

The pastor, who had paused, now went ahead again, faster.

Father Fabre lifted his gun and followed again, wondering if he'd abused the man's sensibilities, some article of the accumulator's creed. He saw a piano stool well suited to his strategy. This he could give up with good grace. "Now here's something," he said. "I wouldn't mind having this." He sounded as though he thought he could get it too.

The pastor glanced back and shook his head. "Belongs upstairs."

"Oh, I see," said Father Fabre submissively. There was no piano in the rectory, unless that, too, was in the pastor's room.

The pastor, obviously pleased with his curate's different tone, stopped to explain. "A lot of this will go upstairs when we're through remodeling."

Father Fabre forgot himself. "*Remodeling?*" he said, and tried to get the pastor to look him in the eye.

The pastor turned away.

Father Fabre, who was suddenly seeing his error, began to reflect upon it. There was no material evidence of remodeling, it was true, but he had impugned the pastor's good intentions. Was there a pastor worth his salt who didn't have improvements in mind, contractors and costs on the brain?

They moved deeper into the interior. Above them the jungle joined itself in places now. Father Fabre passed under the full length of a ski without taking notice of it until confronted by its triangular head, arching down at him. He shied away. Suddenly the pastor stopped. Father Fabre pulled up short, cradling his gun, which he'd been using as a cane. Something coiled on the trail?

"How's this?" said the pastor. He was trying the drawers of a pitiful old sideboard affair with its mirrors out and handles maimed, a poor, blind thing. "Like this?" he said. He seemed to have no idea what they were searching for.

"I need something to type on," Father Fabre said bluntly.

The pastor hit the trail again, somehow leaving the impression that Father Fabre was the one who was being difficult.

They continued to the uttermost end of the basement. Here they were confronted by a small mountain of pamphlets. In the bowels of the mountain something moved.

The pastor's hands shifted on his gun. "They're in there," he whispered, and drew back a pace. He waved Father Fabre to one side, raised the gun, and pumped lead into the pamphlets. *Sput-flub. Sput-flub. Sput-spong-spit.*

Father Fabre reached for his left leg, dropped to his knees, his gun clattering down under him. He grabbed up his trouser leg and saw the little hole bleeding in his calf. It hurt, but not as much as he would've thought.

The pastor came over to examine the leg. He bent down. "Just a flesh wound," he said, straightening up. "You're lucky."

"*Lucky!*"

"Tire there at the bottom of the pile. Absorbed most of the fire power. Bullet went through and ricocheted. You're lucky. Here." The pastor was holding out his hand.

"Oh, no," said Father Fabre, and lowered his trouser leg over the wound.

The pastor seemed to be surprised that Father Fabre wouldn't permit him to pinch the bullet out with his dirty fingers.

Father Fabre stood up. The leg held him, but his walking would be affected. He thought he could feel some blood in his sock. "Afraid I'll have to leave you," he said. He glanced at the pastor, still seeking sympathy. And there it was, at last, showing in the pastor's face, some sympathy, and words were

103

on the way—no, caught again in the log jam of the man's mind and needing a shove if they were to find their way down to the mouth, and so Father Fabre kept on looking at the pastor, shoving . . .

"Sorry it had to happen," muttered the pastor. Apparently that was going to be all. He was picking up Father Fabre's gun.

Painfully, Father Fabre began to walk. Sorry! That it *had* to happen! Anyone else, having fired the shot, would've been only too glad to assume the blame. What kind of man was this? This was a man of very few words, as everyone knew, and he had said he was sorry. How sorry then? Sorry enough?

Father Fabre stopped. "How about this?" he said, sounding as if he hadn't asked about the maple table before. It was a daring maneuver, but he was giving the pastor a chance to reverse himself without losing face, to redeem himself . . .

The pastor was shaking his head.

Father Fabre lost patience. He'd let the old burglar shoot him down and this was what he got for it. "Why not?" he demanded.

The pastor was looking down, not meeting Father Fabre's eye. "You don't have a good easy chair, do you?"

Father Fabre, half turning, saw what the pastor had in mind. There just weren't any words for the chair. Father Fabre regarded it stoically—the dust lying fallow in the little mohair furrows, the ruptured bottom—and didn't know what to say. It would be impossible to convey his true feelings to the pastor. The pastor really did think that this was a good easy chair. There was no way to get at the facts with him. But the proper study of curates is pastors. "It's *too* good," Father Fabre said, making the most of his opportunity. "If I ever sat down in a chair like that I might never get up again. No, it's not for me."

Oh, the pastor was pleased—the man was literally smiling.

Of a self-denying nature himself, famous for it in the diocese, he saw the temptation that such a chair would be to his curate.

"No?" he said, and appeared, besides pleased, relieved.

"No, thanks," said Father Fabre briskly, and moved on. It might be interesting to see how far he could go with the man—but some other time. His leg seemed to be stiffening.

When they arrived back at the door, the pastor, in a manner that struck Father Fabre as too leisurely under the circumstances, racked the guns, hung up his cap, boxed the dust out of his knees and elbows, all the time gazing back where they'd been—not, Father Fabre thought, with the idea of returning to the rats as soon as he decently could, but with the eyes of a game conservationist looking to the future.

"I was thinking I'd better go to the hospital with this," said Father Fabre. He felt he ought to tell the pastor that he didn't intend to let the bullet remain in his leg.

He left the pastor to lock up, and limped out.

"Better take the car," the pastor called after him.

Father Fabre pulled up short. *"Thanks,"* he said, and began to climb the stairs. The hospital was only a few blocks away, but it hadn't occurred to him that he might have walked there. He was losing every trick. Earlier he had imagined the pastor driving him to the hospital, and the scene there when they arrived—how it would be when the pastor's indifference to his curate's leg became apparent to the doctors and nurses, causing their hearts to harden against him. But all this the pastor had doubtless foreseen, and that was why he wasn't going along. The man was afraid of public opinion.

At the hospital, however, they only laughed when Father Fabre told them what had happened to him, and when, after they had taken the bullet out, he asked if they had to report the matter to the police. Just laughed at him. Only a flesh wound, they said. They didn't even want him to keep off the leg. It had been a mistake for him to ask. Laughed. Told him just to change his sock. But he arranged for the pastor to get the bill. And, on leaving, although he knew nothing would come of it, he said, "I thought you were required by law to report *all* gunshot cases."

When he returned to the rectory, the pastor and John were talking softly in the upstairs hall. They said nothing to him, which he thought strange, and so he said nothing to them. He was lucky, he guessed, that they hadn't laughed. He limped into his room, doubting whether John had even been told, and closed the door with a little bang. He turned and stood still. Then, after a few moments in which he realized why the pastor and John were in the hall, he limped over to the window— to the old mohair chair.

Ruefully, he recalled his false praise of the chair. How it had cost him! For the pastor had taken him at his word. After the shooting accident, the pastor must have been in no mood to give Father Fabre a table in which he seemed only half interested. Nothing would do then but that the wounded curate be compensated with the object of his only enthusiasm in the basement. No one knew better than the pastor where soft living could land a young priest, and yet there it was— luxury itself, procured by the pastor and dragged upstairs by his agent and now awaiting his curate's pleasure. And to think it might have been the maple table!

They clearly hadn't done a thing to the chair. The dust was all there, every grain intact. They were waiting for him, the pastor and John, waiting to see him sitting in it. He thought of disappointing them, of holing up as the pastor had earlier. But he just couldn't contend with the man any more that day. He didn't know how he'd ever be able to thank them, John for carrying it up from the basement, the pastor for the thing it- self, but he limped over to the door to let them in. Oh, it was a losing game.

DEFECTION OF A FAVORITE

I was waiting in the lobby, sitting in a fairly clean overshoe, out of the draft and near a radiator, dozing, when the monthly meeting of the ushers ended and the men began to drift up from the church basement. Once a meeting got under way, the majority of the ushers, as well as Father Malt, their old pastor, liked to wind it up and break for the rectory, for pinochle and beer. Father Malt, seeing me, called "Fritz!" and I came, crossing in front of Mr. Cormack, the new man, who muttered "Bad luck!" and blessed himself. I hadn't thought much about him before, but this little action suggested to me that his eyes were failing or that he was paranoidal, for, though a black cat, I have a redeeming band of white at my throat.

While I waited for the ushers to put their hats and coats on, I thought I saw their souls reflected in their mufflers, in those warm, unauthentic plaids and soiled white rayons and nylons, a few with fringe work, some worn as chokers in the nifty, or *haute*-California, manner, and some tucked in between coat and vest in a way that may be native to our part of Minnesota.

Father Malt and I went out the door together. Going barefooted, as nature intended, I was warned of the old ice beneath the new-fallen snow. Father Malt, however, in shoes and overshoes, walked blindly, and slipped and fell.

107

When several ushers took hold of Father Malt, Mr. Keller, the head usher, a druggist and a friend of physicians, spoke with authority. "Don't move him! That's the worst thing you can do! Call an ambulance!"

Three ushers thought to cover Father Malt with their overcoats (three others, too late with theirs, held them in their hands), and everyone just stood and stared, as I did, at the old priest, my friend and protector, lying under the mound of overcoats, with the indifferent snow settling down as upon a new grave. I began to feel the cold in my bones and to think that I should certainly perish if I were locked out on such a night. I heard Mr. Keller ordering Mr. Cormack to the rectory to phone for an ambulance. Reluctantly—not through any deficiency in my sorrow—I left the scene of the accident, crossed the snowy lawn, and entered the rectory with Mr. Cormack.

After Mr. Cormack had summoned an ambulance, he called his old pastor, Father O'Hannon, of St. Clara's, Minneapolis (of which Sherwood, our town, was gradually becoming a suburb), and asked him to be at the hospital, in case Father Malt should be in danger of death and in need of extreme unction. "The assistant here, Father Burner, isn't around. His car's gone from the garage, and there's no telling when that one'll be back," said Mr. Cormack, sounding lonesome for his old parish. At St. Clara's, he'd evidently been on more intimate terms with the priests. His last words to Father O'Hannon, "We could sure use someone like you out here," gave me the idea that he had gone fishing for Father Burner's favor but had caught one of the white whale's flukes. Now, like so many of us, he dreamed of getting even someday. I could only wish him luck as he left the rectory.

I watched at the window facing upon the tragedy, enduring the cold draft there for Father Malt's sake, until the ambulance came. Then I retired to the parlor register and soon fell asleep

—not without a prayer for Father Malt and many more for myself. With Father Burner running the rectory, it was going to be a hard, hard, and possibly fatal winter for me.

The ironic part was that Father Burner and I, bad as he was, had a lot in common. We disliked the same people (Mr. Keller, for instance), we disliked the same dishes (those suited to Father Malt's dentures), but, alas, we also disliked each other. This fault originated in Father Burner's raw envy of me—which, however, I could understand. Father Malt didn't improve matters when he referred to me before visitors, in Father Burner's presence, as *the* assistant. I was realist enough not to hope for peace between us assistants as long as Father Malt lived. But it did seem a shame that there was no way of letting Father Burner know I was prepared—if and when his position improved—to be his friend and favorite, although not necessarily in that order. (For some reason, I seem to make a better favorite than friend.) As it was Father Burner's misfortune to remain a curate too long, it was mine to know that my life of privilege—my preferred place at table, for example—appeared to operate at the expense of his rights and might be the cause of my ultimate undoing. It was no good wishing, as I sometimes did, that Father Malt were younger—he was eighty-one —or that I were older, that we two could pass on together when the time came.

Along toward midnight, waking, I heard Father Burner's car pull into the driveway. A moment later the front porch cracked under his heavy step. He entered the rectory, galoshes and all, and, as was his custom, proceeded to foul his own nest wherever he went, upstairs and down. Finally, after looking, as he always did, for the telephone messages that seemingly never came, or, as he imagined, never got taken down, he went out on the front porch and brought in more snow and the evening paper. He sat reading in the parlor—it was then midnight—still in his dripping galoshes, still in perfect ignorance of what had befallen Father Malt *and* me. Before he arrived, the telephone had been ringing at half-hour intervals—obviously the hospital, or one of the ushers, trying to reach him. The next time, I knew, it would toll for me.

Although I could see no way to avoid my fate, I did see the folly of waiting up for it. I left the parlor to Father Burner and went to the kitchen, where I guessed he would look last for me, if he knew anything of my habits, for I seldom entered there and never stayed long. Mrs. Wynn, the housekeeper, loosely speaking, was no admirer of mine, nor I of her womanly disorder.

I concealed myself in a basket of clean, or at least freshly laundered, clothes, and presently, despite everything, I slept.

Early the following day, when Father Burner came downstairs, he had evidently heard the news, but he was late for his Mass, as usual, and had time for only one wild try at me with his foot. However, around noon, when he returned from the hospital, he paused only to phone the chancery to say that Father Malt had a fractured hip and was listed as "critical" and promptly chased me from the front of the house to the kitchen. He'd caught me in the act of exercising my claws on his new brief case, which lay on the hall chair. The brief case was a present to himself at Christmas—no one else thought quite so much of him—but he hadn't been able to find a real use for it and I think it piqued him to see that I had.

"I want that black devil kept out of my sight," he told Mrs. Wynn, before whom he was careful to watch his language.

That afternoon I heard him telling Father Ed Desmond, his friend from Minneapolis, who'd dropped by, that he favored the wholesale excommunication of household pets from homes and particularly from rectories. He mentioned me in the same breath with certain parrots and hamsters he was familiar with. Although he was speaking on the subject of clutter, he said nothing about model railroads, Father Desmond's little vice, or about photography, his own. The term "household pet" struck me as a double-barreled euphemism, unpetted as I was and denied the freedom of the house.

And still, since I'd expected to be kicked out into the weather, and possibly not to get that far alive, I counted my deportation to the kitchen as a blessing—a temporary one, however. I had no reason to believe that Father Burner's feeling about me had changed. I looked for something new in persecutions. When nothing happened, I looked all the harder.

I spent my days in the kitchen with Mrs. Wynn, sleeping when I could, just hanging around in her way when I couldn't. If I wearied of that, as I inevitably did, I descended into the cellar. The cellar smelled of things too various—laundry, coal, developing fluid, and mice—and the unseemly noise of the home-canned goods digesting on the shelves, which another might never notice, reached and offended my ears. After an hour down there, where the floor was cold to my feet, I was ready to return to the kitchen and Mrs. Wynn.

Mrs. Wynn had troubles of her own—her husband hit the jar—but they did nothing to Christianize her attitude toward me. She fed me scraps, and kicked me around, not hard but regularly, in the course of her work. I expected little from her, however. She was another in the long tradition of unjust stewards.

Father Burner's relatively civil conduct was harder to comprehend. One afternoon, rising from sleep and finding the kitchen door propped open, I forgot myself and strolled into the parlor, into his very presence. He was reading *Church Property Administration*, a magazine I hadn't seen in the house before. Having successfully got that far out of line—as far as the middle of the room—I decided to keep going. As if by chance, I came to my favorite register, where, after looking about to estimate the shortest distance between me and any suitable places of refuge in the room, I collapsed around the heat. There was still no intimation of treachery—only peace surpassing all understanding, only the rush of warmth from the register, the winds of winter outside, and the occasional click and whisper of a page turning in *Church Property Administration.*

Not caring to push my luck, wishing to come and doze another day, wanting merely to establish a precedent, I got up and strolled back into the kitchen—to think. I threw out the possibility that Father Burner had suffered a lapse of memory, had forgotten the restriction placed on my movements. I conceived the idea that he'd lost, or was losing, his mind, and then, grudgingly, I gave up the idea. He was not trying to ignore me. He was ignoring me without trying. I'd been doing the same thing to people for years, but I'd never dreamed that one of them would do it to me.

From that day on, I moved freely about the house, as I had in Father Malt's time, and Mrs. Wynn, to add to the mystery, made no effort to keep me with her in the kitchen. I was thus in a position to observe other lapses or inconsistencies in Father Burner. Formerly, he'd liked to have lights burning all over the house. Now that he was paying the bill, the place was often shrouded in darkness. He threw out the tattered rugs at the front and back doors and bought rubber mats—at a saving, evidently, for although one mat bore the initial "B," the other had an "R," which stood for nobody but may have been the closest thing he could get to go with the "B." I noticed, too, that he took off his galoshes before entering the house, as though it were no longer just church property but home to him.

I noticed that he was going out less with his camera, and to

112

the hospital more, not just to visit Father Malt, to whom he'd never had much to say, but to visit the sick in general.

In former times, he had been loath to go near the hospital during the day, and at night, before he'd leave his bed to make a sick call, there had had to be infallible proof that a patient was in danger of death. It had been something awful to hear him on the line with the hospital in the wee hours, haggling, asking if maybe they weren't a little free and easy with their designation "critical," as, indeed, I believe some of them liked to be. He'd tried to get them to change a patient's "critical" to "fair" (which meant he could forget about that one), and acted as though there were some therapeutic power about the word, if the hospital could just be persuaded to make use of it. Father Malt, with his hearing aid off, was virtually deaf, Mrs. Wynn roomed down the street, and so I had been the one to suffer. "Oh, go on, go on," I'd wanted to say. "Go on over there, or don't go—but hang up! Some of us want to sleep!" There were nights when I'd hardly sleep a wink—unlike Father Burner, who, even if he *did* go to the hospital, would come bumbling back and drop off with his clothes on.

In general, I now found his attitude toward his duties altered, but not too much so, not extreme. If he'd had a night of sick calls, he'd try to make up for it with a nap before dinner. His trouble was still a pronounced unwillingness to take a total loss on sacrifice.

I found other evidence of the change he was undergoing— outlines of sermons in the wastebasket, for instance. In the past, he'd boasted that he thought of whatever he was going to say on Sunday in the time it took him to walk from the altar to the pulpit. He was not afraid to speak on the parishioners' duty to contribute generously to the support of the church, a subject neglected under Father Malt, who'd been satisfied with what the people wanted to give—very little. Father Burner tried to get them interested in the church. He said it was a matter of pride—pride in the good sense of the word. I felt he went too far, however, when, one Sunday, he told the congregation that it was their church *and* their rectory. There had always been too many converts hanging around the house for instruction, and now there were more of them than in Father Malt's day. The house just wasn't large enough for all of us.

Father Desmond, noting how little time Father Burner now had for himself (and for Father Desmond), suggested that the chancery be petitioned for help ("There's just too much work here for one man, Ernest"), but Father Burner said no, and so resisted what must have been the worst of all possible temptations to him, the assistant's sweet dream—to have an assistant. He said he'd go it alone. It almost seemed as if he were out to distinguish himself, not in the eyes of others— something he'd always worked at—but in his own eyes.

At any rate, he was beginning to act and talk like a real pastor. When Father Desmond came over or phoned, they talked of construction and repairs. Father Desmond, one of our most promising young pastors, was building a new school —with undue emphasis, it seemed to me, on the gymnasium. Father Burner, lacking authority to do more, made needed repairs. He had the rectory kitchen painted and purchased a Mixmaster for Mrs. Wynn. He had the windows in the church basement calked and installed a small institutional kitchen there, thus showing all too clearly that he intended to go in for parish suppers, which he'd abominated in the past as the hardest part of the priesthood.

Father Desmond and Father Burner now spoke fluently a gibberish that only a building pastor could comprehend. They talked of organs, bells, and bulletin boards, coin counters, confessional chairs and hearing devices, flooring, kneeler pads, gym seats, radiation, filing systems, electric fans, mops, and brooms, and all by their difficult trade names—Wurlitzer, Carillonic, Confessionaire, Confession-Ease, Speed Sweep, the Klopp (coin counter); Vakumatic, Scrubber-Vac, Kardex, Mopmaster, and many more. And shrubbery and trees.

There was a great need for trees in Sherwood—a need that, I daresay, had never occurred to Father Malt, or, presumably, to many of the older inhabitants of the town. The new people, who lived in "ranch houses" and worked in Minneapolis, seemed to like trees, and so, in his new phase, did Father Burner.

"When spring comes," he said, in cold January, "I'll plant some maples."

Father Desmond, who knew where Father Burner's thoughts were hiding, said, "Someday you'll build, too, Ernest."

After fourteen months in the hospital, Father Malt was moved to the sisters' infirmary in St. Paul, where there were supposed to be other patients, including old priests, of similar tastes and outlook. In our busy rectory, the seasons had come and gone without pause, the seasons as we observed them— baseball, football, Christmas, basketball, and Lent again. There were further improvements, or at least changes. Father Burner got Mrs. Wynn a white radio for her kitchen and thereby broke the tradition of silence we'd had under Father Malt, who hadn't even listened to Cedric Adams and the ten o'clock news.

I spent my mornings in the parlor and thus escaped the full effect of Mrs. Wynn's programs, but in the parlor, or wherever I went in the house, I heard those same voices, always at the same hour, always repeating themselves, and for a while, at first, I took a certain interest in those miserable lives. Can a woman over thirty-five find love again? Should a girl, the ward of a man twenty years older, marry him? For these questions, as time went on, I could see there would be no answers.

In our rectory, another question was being asked, and for this question there had to be an answer. Father Burner was pastor of the church in all but name, and could hope, with good reason, that this, too, would be added unto him in time, if he worked and prayed hard enough. During the first weeks after the accident, Father Burner and Father Desmond had discussed the physical aspects of Father Malt's case—what kind of cast, the number and type of pins, and all the rest. Lately, however, they'd been taking another line, more to the point and touching upon Father Burner's chances.

The difficulty lay, of course, in Father Malt's refusal to give himself up to the life of an invalid. Nothing could be done about appointing his successor until he actually resigned or died. No one, of course, openly suggested that he do either. It was up to him to decide. Father Desmond believed that, sooner or later, the Archbishop would go to Father Malt and precipitate a solution of the problem. But even the Archbishop was powerless to force Father Malt to resign against his will. As long as Father Malt wished, as long as he lived, he would be pastor, and this was according to canon law. Father Malt was an "irremovable pastor," well liked by the people of the parish, a favorite at the chancery, where, however, it was known—according to Father Desmond—that Father Burner was doing a bang-up job.

Father Burner was the rare one who hadn't asked for help, who was going it alone, with just two monks, down from St. John's, to assist him over weekends. He would go on retreat in June for five days (he wasn't much on card games, though), but he planned no regular vacation. He worked like a dog. He lost weight. He was tired. I was edified.

In May, I heard Father Desmond say, "Ernest, it's time to widen your circle of friends," and so Father Burner, rather unwillingly, tried to give a poker party at the rectory. Father

Desmond, popular (as Father Burner wasn't) with the older men, a surprising number of whom claimed to have sold him on sobriety, invited several pastors and, significantly, no curates. But only two of those invited showed up—Father Kling and Father Moore. They belonged to the active set, a kind of Jockey Club for pastors, which maintained a floating poker game, a duckblind, and a summer lodge. They gambled, hunted, and fished in common.

On the evening of the party, when they came into the dining room, where the cards and chips were laid out, I could see that Father Desmond had led them to believe that Father Burner, of all people, was playing host to an almost official session. Father Kling, a forceful man, glanced at Father Moore, a mild one, and remarked that he'd understood others were coming. With good grace, however, he and Father Moore sat down to play.

Father Desmond, who seemed to regard his function as essentially one of public relations, started right in to plump for Father Burner. "It's a shame somebody doesn't tell the old man to retire," he said, referring to Father Malt. "It's not fair to Ernest, here, and it's not fair to the parish. This place needs a young man, with young ideas." I, for one, wasn't surprised by the utter silence that followed these remarks. Father Kling and Father Moore, as even Father Desmond should've known, were not so young themselves, nor were they so hot on young ideas.

Father Burner wisely stayed out of it. Father Desmond continued along the same lines, however, until Father Kling commented dryly, "It's his hip, not his mind, that's gone wrong, isn't it?" and drained his highball.

"He's had quite a time of it, hasn't he?" said Father Moore gently. "Poor Dutch."

"How about poor Ernest?" asked Father Desmond.

117

"Uh, yes, of course," said Father Moore.

Father Desmond seemed to realize that he was doing no good and shut up. At least he might have waited, I thought, until they were feeling better. Father Kling had a little pile in front of him, and perhaps he'd remember where he got it. That was the only thing in Father Burner's favor when Mrs. Wynn came into the dining room and announced the Archbishop and another priest.

I followed Father Burner out of the dining room, but stopped at the door to the parlor, into which Mrs. Wynn had shown the guests. I preferred to enter unobserved.

When Father Burner attempted to kiss the episcopal ring, the Archbishop put his hand behind him. He reserved the ring-kissing business for ceremonial occasions, as everyone knew, but it was customary to make a try for it.

At Father Burner's invitation, the Archbishop and his companion, a young priest whose eyes looked as though he'd been driving all day, sat down, and at that juncture Father Desmond and the two other poker players came in to declare themselves. While they, too, tried to get at the Archbishop's ring, I slipped into the parlor unseen and then along the wall until I came to the library table. There, back out of view, at the intersection of the crossbars supporting the table, I took up my position.

The Archbishop said that they'd been passing the church, on their way back from a confirmation tour along the northern marches of the diocese, when he thought of dropping in on Father Burner.

"It's good to see you all together," he said, looking them over. He liked to have his priests associating with one another, I knew, and not seeking other company to excess—except, of course, when necessary at parish functions.

The Archbishop asked about Father Malt (I daresay His

118

Excellency, of those present, had seen him last), and Father
Burner and Father Desmond, replying, sounded a little too
broken up to suit my taste, or to sound much like themselves.

When the conversation came around to Father Burner and
the fine work he was doing, Father Desmond ran it into the
ground. He fed the most leading questions to Father Burner,
who expressed himself well, I thought, although referring too
often to the Archbishop for a higher opinion on trivial matters.
It galled me to see Father Desmond turning the occasion into
a grease job all around. Father Burner, possibly recognizing
this but not able to turn Father Desmond off, excused himself
and went down the hallway to the kitchen.

Father Desmond, speaking in a near whisper, as if he were
telling a secret, said, "You know, Your Excellency, Father's
taken some nice shots of the Cathedral at night. If you'd care
to see them . . ."

"I believe I've seen them," said the Archbishop. He was
looking over Father Desmond's shoulder, disapprovingly, at
his own smiling picture on the wall—not one of Father Burner's
shots, however.

"Yes," said Father Desmond. "But he doesn't have time for
much any more."

The Archbishop nodded, and got up from his chair. "Excuse
me, Father," he said. He crossed the room to the bookcase.

Mrs. Wynn entered the parlor with a tray of wineglasses,
which she placed on the table.

Father Burner followed her with a bottle. I was happy to
see that he'd had good luck with the cork. Later on, when the
Archbishop had left, they'd switch back to bourbon (except
Father Desmond, who was on 7-Up). For some reason, sacramental wine, taken daily, spoiled them for other wines.

"This is hardly the time, but it may be the place to ask you,"
said Father Burner, handing the Archbishop his glass, "but

119

with Father Malt off the scene, Your Excellency, I was wondering if I dare go ahead with a tuck-pointing job on the church. I've been considering it—only academically, that is, Your Excellency, because it'll run into quite a lot of money." The Archbishop was silent. Father Burner started up again, in a manner feeble for him. "In the pastor's temporary absence, the disposition of these matters . . ."

"Couldn't it wait a bit, Father?" asked the Archbishop. It was a tense moment, a difficult reply indeed, when one tried to analyze it, as I did. At its best, it could mean that Father Burner would soon be empowered to make decisions concerning the church; at its worst, it could mean that the Archbishop expected Father Malt to recover and take over again, or, what was most likely, that he was not considering the question at all, regarded it as out of order, ill-timed, and impertinent. I felt that the Archbishop understood the reason for it, however. Father Burner had been overwhelmed by the visit, and flattered that others, particularly Father Kling and Father Moore, should be present to witness it. Such a visit—not an official visitation—could be enough to make him. It had been a great night for Father Burner until he popped that question.

When, a few minutes later, the Archbishop got up to leave, I came out from under the library table, went over to Father Burner, and brushed up against his trouser leg, purring.

The Archbishop, hearing me, I think, before he saw me, gazed down and said, "Do you like animals, Father?"

"Yes, Your Excellency," said Father Burner, who was only a dog-lover at best, and where I was concerned, I know, his answer was a barefaced lie—until he made it. From that moment on—there was no doubt of it—he loved me.

"This one, I see, likes you," said the Archbishop, smiling. "Some believe it to be an infallible sign, the best of character references."

120

Father Burner blushed and said, "I wish I could believe in that sign, Your Excellency."

I trotted over to the Archbishop, selected his black trouser leg from all the others, and brushed against it, nicely purring. Everyone laughed.

"*Credo!*" cried Father Burner.

I was not surprised when, on the following morning, Father Burner invited me to join him at table for breakfast. I had wanted my elevation to my former place to happen of itself, to be a voluntary act on Father Burner's part, as mine had been on his account, and for that reason, and because I wanted Mrs. Wynn to get a good eyeful, I'd remained in the kitchen, awaiting, as it were, my nomination. After offering Mass, Father Burner came and sought me.

"Where's Fritz?" he asked.

"Who?" said Mrs. Wynn.

"Fritz," Father Burner said. "My cat."

"Oh, him," said Mrs. Wynn, who, it occurred to me, represented the sort of person who could live in the thick of history and never know the difference.

I walked out from under the kitchen table. Father Burner knelt and lifted me into his arms. He carried me into the dining room and pulled my old chair away from the wall and up to the table. We both sat down—to what I hoped would be only the first of many pleasant meals together.

I ate my bacon right royally and ruminated on the events of the evening before. I could not honestly say that I'd planned the splendid thing I'd done. It had more or less happened— unless, of course, I was both kinder and wiser than I believed myself to be. I was eating high on the hog again, I had my rightful place back, my reward for patience, and I was only sorry that Father Burner still had to wait for his. His buds had been pinched off at the start, but his roots had grown strong and deep. If he managed to flower, he'd be the classic type of late-blooming pastor. Until then he had me at his side, to him everything I'd been to Father Malt—friend and favorite, and, more, the very symbol and prefigurement of power. I actually liked him, I discovered. I liked him for what I'd done for him. But why had I done it? I didn't really know why. I work at times in ways so inscrutable that even I cannot tell what good or evil I am up to.

Before we'd finished breakfast, Father Desmond phoned— to discuss the Archbishop's visit, I gathered, for Father Burner said, "I've decided not to talk any more about it, Ed." I could almost hear Father Desmond squawking, "Whatta ya mean, Ernest?" "Maybe that's part of the trouble," Father Burner said. "We're talkin' it to death." Evidently Father Desmond took offense at that, for Father Burner spoke quickly, out of context. "Why don't you come for dinner sometime, Ed? When? Well, come tomorrow. Come early. Good."

Father Burner hung up, bounced over to the table, chucked me fondly behind the ears, took a banana out of the fruit bowl, and went whistling off to his car—off to do the work of the parish, to return a defective length of hose, to visit the sick and pregnant, to drive to Minneapolis for more informal conferences with building experts, lay and clerical. He had several projects going ahead—academically, that is: the tuck pointing, a new decorating job inside the church, and outside, possibly, a floodlight on the dome, which I thought a paltry affair better left in the dark.

Before lunch that day, he returned with a half dozen mousetraps. He seemed to want me to follow him around the house, and therefore I attended him most faithfully, while he set the traps in what he regarded as likely places. I rather expected to be jollied about my indifference to mousing. There was none of that, however, and what might have been an embarrassing experience for me became instead an occasion of instruction. Using a pencil for a mouse, Father Burner showed me how the trap worked, which was quite unnecessary but a nice gesture, I thought.

That evening—with Father Burner still in the mood to exterminate—we appeared together for the first time in public, at the monthly meeting of the ushers. In the future, Father Burner announced, all notices of the sort now being posted on the bulletin board at the rear of the church would have to emanate from his office (which, strictly speaking, was his bedroom) and carry his signature. This was a cruel but unavoidable check to Mr. Keller, who had become too prolific for his own good. He used the drugstore typewriter and special engraved cards bearing his name and title, and he took an authoritarian tone in matters of etiquette ("Keep your feet off the kneelers," "Don't stand in the back of the church," "Ask the usher to find you a seat—that's what he's there for," etc.), and in other matters (Lost and Found, old-clothes collections, ticket sales, and the like) he made it sound as though these were all services and causes thought up and sponsored by him personally. I felt that he was not far from posting bargains in real estate, another means of livelihood for him at the drugstore, when Father Burner stepped in. Mr. Keller took it well—too well, I thought. He murmured a few meek words about trying to spare Father Burner the trouble, as he'd spared Father Malt the trouble. (He now visited Father Malt regularly at the infirmary.) Before we left, he asked Father Burner to lead the ushers in the usual prayer for Father Malt's swift recovery.

It was early afternoon the next day when Father Burner remembered the mousetraps. I accompanied him on his rounds, but there was nothing I liked about the business before us.

First we went to the pantry and kitchen, where Mrs. Wynn constantly dropped and mislaid quantities of food. Any mouse caught in a trap there, I thought, deserved to die for his gluttony. None had. In the cellar, however, Father Burner had snared two young ones, both from a large family whose members I saw from time to time. My record with them had been good, and they, in turn, had played fair with me and had committed no obvious depredations to make me look bad. When their loss was noted, the others, I feared, would blame me—not for the crime itself but for letting it happen within my precinct.

Father Burner removed the little bodies from the traps, and then, with the best of intentions and with a smile, which only made it worse, he did a terrible thing. He extended a hand to me, a hand curled in kindness, inviting me to banquet on the remains. I turned away in a swoon, physically sick and sick at heart. I made my way upstairs, wanting to be alone. I considered bitterly others I'd known and trusted in the past. Always, except with Father Malt, when I'd persuaded myself to take a chance on one of them, there'd be something like this. I tried to forget, or to sleep it off, which proved impossible. I knew what I had to do before I could begin to forget, and so I did it. I forgave Father Burner. It was another lesson in charity, one that cost me more than my going to bat for him with the Archbishop, but I'm afraid it was entirely lost on him.

Father Desmond came for dinner that afternoon at four, which I thought rather early even for "early." When he arrived, I was in the front hall having a go at the brief case. He went right past me. I could see that he had something on his mind.

"I just couldn't stay away," he said, taking a chair across

from Father Burner in the parlor. "I've got what I *think* is good news, Ernest."

Father Burner glanced up from *Church Property Adminis-tration* and shook his head. "I don't want to hear it," he said, "if it's about you-know-what."

"I'll just tell you what I *know* to be true," Father Desmond said, "and let it go at that."

"Whatever it is, it can wait," said Father Burner. I could see, however, that he'd listen if he was primed again.

Father Desmond bore down on him. "Sure, I know, you'll get it in the mail—when you get it. That's what you figure. I admire your restraint, Ernest, but let's not be superstitious about it, either."

Father Burner, sprawling in his chair, rolled and unrolled *Church Property Administration*. Then, making a tube of it, he put it to his eye and peered through it, down his black leg, a great distance, and appeared finally to sight the silver glow on the toe of his big black shoe, which lay in the sunlight. "All right, Ed," he said. "Let's have it."

"All right, then," said Father Desmond. "Here it is. I have it on reliable authority—that is to say, my spies tell me—the Archbishop visited the infirmary today." I interpreted "spies" to mean some little nun or other on whom Father Desmond bestowed sample holy cards.

Father Burner, taking a long-suffering tone in which there was just a touch of panic, said, "Ed, you know he does that all the time. You'll have to do better than that."

Father Desmond tried to come up with more. "He had *words* with Dutch."

Father Burner flung himself out of his chair. He engaged in swordplay with the air, using *Church Property Administra-tion*. "How do you mean 'he had words'? You don't mean to say they quarreled?"

125

Father Desmond could only reply, "I just mean they talked at *some* length."

Father Burner gave a great snort and threw *Church Property Administration* across the room. It clattered against the bookcase, a broken sword. He wheeled and walked the floor, demanding, "Then why'd you say they had words? Why make something out of nothing? Why not tell it straight, Ed? Just once, huh?" He was standing over Father Desmond.

"You're under a strain, Ernest," said Father Desmond, getting up from his chair. "Maybe I shouldn't have said anything about it at all."

Father Burner stared at him. "*Said?* Said *what?* That's just it, Ed—you haven't said anything." He took another walk around the room, saying the word "nothing" over and over to himself.

Father Desmond cut in, "All right, Ernest, I'm sorry," and sat down in his chair.

Then Father Burner, too, sat down, and both men were overcome by quiet and perhaps shame. Several minutes passed. I was sorry for Father Burner. He'd sacrificed his valuable silence to his curiosity and received nothing in return.

I addressed the brief case, making my claws catch and pop in the soft, responsive leather. I wished that I were plucking instead at the top of Father Desmond's soft head.

Father Desmond glanced over at me and then at Father Burner.

"Why do you let him do that?" he asked.

"He likes to."

"Yeah?" said Father Desmond. "Does he ever bring you a mouse?"

With one paw poised, I listened for Father Burner's answer.

"You don't see any around, do you?" he said.

Well done, I thought, and renewed my attack on the brief

case. I had the feeling that Father Desmond still wanted to tell the world what he'd do to me if it were his brief case, but, if so, he denied himself and got out a cigar.

"What'd you think of the plans for that rectory in South Dakota?" he asked.

"Not bad," said Father Burner, looking around for his *Church Property Administration*.

"There it is," said Father Desmond, as if it were always misplacing itself. He went over by the bookcase, picked up the magazine, and delivered it to Father Burner.

I curled up to nap. I could see that they were going to have one of their discussions.

When I heard the back door open, I supposed it was Mrs. Wynn coming in to start dinner, but it was Mr. Keller. I saw him advancing gravely up the hallway, toward me, carrying a traveling bag that I recognized as one the ushers had given Father Malt. Instantly I concluded that Father Malt had passed away in the night, that the nuns had failed to inform Father Burner, and had instead told Mr. Keller, the faithful visitor, to whom they'd also entrusted the deceased's few belongings.

Mr. Keller set down the bag and, without looking into the parlor, started back the way he'd come, toward the back door. Father Burner and Father Desmond, at the sight of the bag, seemed unable to rise from their chairs, powerless to speak.

After a moment, I saw Father Malt emerging from the kitchen, on crutches, followed by Mr. Keller. He worked his way up the hallway, talking to himself. "Somebody painted my kitchen," I heard him say.

I beheld him as one risen from the dead. He looked the same to me but different—an imperfect reproduction of himself as I recalled him, imperfect only because he appeared softer, whiter, and, of course, because of the crutches.

127

Not seeing me by the hatrack, he clumped into the parlor, nodded familiarly to Father Burner and Father Desmond, and said, again to himself, "Somebody changed my chairs around."

Father Desmond suddenly shot up from his chair, said, "I gotta go," and went. Mr. Keller seemed inclined to stick around. Father Burner, standing, waited for Father Malt to come away from the library table, where he'd spotted some old copies of *Church Property Administration.*

Father Malt thrust his hand under the pile of magazines, weighed it, and slowly, with difficulty, turned on his crutches, to face Father Burner.

They stared at each other, Father Malt and Father Burner, like two popes themselves not sure which one was real.

I decided to act. I made my way to the center of the room and stood between them. I sensed them both looking at me, then *to* me—for a sign. Canon law itself was not more clear, more firm, than the one I lived by. I turned my back on Father Burner, went over to Father Malt, and favored him with a solemn purr and dubbed his trouser leg lightly with my tail, reversing the usual course of prerogative between lord and favorite, switching the current of power. With a purr, I'd restored Father Malt's old authority in the house. Of necessity—authority as well as truth being one and indivisible—I'd unmade Father Burner. I was sorry for him.

He turned and spoke harshly to Mr. Keller. "Why don't you go see if you left the back door open?"

When Father Burner was sure that Mr. Keller had gone, he faced Father Malt. The irremovable pastor stood perspiring on his crutches. As long as he lived, he had to be pastor, I saw; his need was the greater. And Father Burner saw it, too. He went up to Father Malt, laid a strong, obedient hand on the old one that held tight to the right crutch, and was then the man he'd been becoming.

"Hello, boss," he said. "Glad you're back."

It was his finest hour. In the past, he had lacked the will to accept his setbacks with grace and had derived no merit from them. It was difficult to believe that he'd profited so much from my efforts in his behalf—my good company and constant example. I was happy for him.

ZEAL

South of St. Paul the conductor appeared at the head of the coach, held up his ticket punch, and clicked it.

The Bishop felt for his ticket. It was there.

"I know it's not a pass," said Father Early. He had been talking across the aisle to one of the pilgrims he was leading to Rome, but now he was back on the subject of the so-called clergy pass. "But it is a privilege."

The Bishop said nothing. He'd meant to imply by his silence before, when Father Early brought up the matter, that there was nothing wrong with an arrangement which permitted the clergy to travel in parlor cars at coach rates. The Bishop wished the arrangement were in effect in all parts of the country, and on all trains.

"But on a run like this, Bishop, with these fine coaches, I I daresay there aren't many snobs who'll go to the trouble of filling out the form."

The Bishop looked away. Father Early had a nose like a parrot's and something on it like psoriasis that held the Bishop's attention—unfortunately, for Father Early seemed to think it was his talk. The Bishop had a priest or two in his diocese like Father Early.

130

"Oh, the railroads, I daresay, mean well."

"Yes," said the Bishop distantly. The voice at his right ear went on without him. He gazed out the window, up at the limestone scarred by its primeval intercourse with the Mississippi, now shrunk down into itself, and there he saw a cave, another cave, and another. Criminals had been discovered in them, he understood, and ammunition from the Civil War, and farther down the river, in the high bluffs, rattlesnakes were said to be numerous still.

"Bishop, I don't think I'm one to strain at a gnat." (The Bishop glanced at Father Early's nose with interest.) "But I must say I fear privilege more than persecution. Of course the one follows the other, as the night the day."

"Is it true, Father, that there are rattlesnakes along here?"

"Very likely," said Father Early, hardly bothering to look out the window. "Bishop, I was dining in New York, in a crowded place, observed by all and sundry, when the management tried to present me with a bottle of wine. Well!"

The Bishop, spying a whole row of caves, thought of the ancient Nile. Here, though, the country was too fresh and frigid. Here the desert fathers would've married early and gone fishing. The aborigines, by their fruits, pretty much proved that. He tried again to interrupt Father Early. "There must be a cave for you up there, somewhere, Father."

Father Early responded with a laugh that sounded exactly like ha-ha, no more or less. "I'll tell you a secret, Bishop. When I was in seminary, they called me Crazy Early. I understand they still do. Perhaps you knew."

"No," said the Bishop. Father Early flattered himself. The Bishop had never heard of him until that day.

"I thought perhaps Monsignor Reed had told you."

"I seldom see him." He saw Reed only by accident, at somebody's funeral or jubilee celebration or, it seemed, in railroad

stations, which had happened again in Minneapolis that morning. It was Reed who had introduced Father Early to him
then. Had Reed known what he was doing? It was six hours
to Chicago, hours of this . . .

"I suppose you know Macaulay's *England,* Bishop."

"No." There was something to be gained by a frank admission of ignorance when it was assumed anyway.

"Read the section dealing with the status of the common
clergy in the eighteenth century. I'm talking about the Angli-
can clergy. Hardly the equal of servants, knaves, figures of
fun! The fault of the Reformation, you say? Yes, of course"—
the Bishop had in no way signified assent—"but I say it could
happen anywhere, everywhere, any time! Take what's going
on in parts of Europe today. When you consider the status of
the Church there in the past, and the overwhelmingly Catholic
population even now. I wonder, though, if it doesn't take
something to bring us to our senses from time to time—*now*
what do you say, Bishop?"

If the conductor hadn't been upon them, the Bishop
would've said there was probably less danger of the clergy
getting above themselves than there was of their being accepted for less than they were; or at least for less than they
were supposed to be; or was that what Father Early was
saying?

The conductor took up their tickets, placed two receipts
overhead, one white and one blue. Before he moved on, he
advised the Bishop to bring his receipt with him, the blue
one, when he moved into the parlor car.

The Bishop nodded serenely.

Beside him, Father Early was full of silence, and opening
his breviary.

The Bishop, who had expected to be told apologetically that
it was a matter of no importance if he'd used his clergy pass,

had an uncomfortable feeling that Father Early was praying for him.

At Winona, the train stopped for a minute. The Bishop from his window saw Father Early on the platform below talking to an elderly woman. In parting, they pecked at each other, and she handed him a box. Returning to his seat, he said he'd had a nice visit with his sister. He went to the head of the coach with the box, and came slowly back down the aisle, offering the contents to the pilgrims. "Divinity? Divinity?" The Bishop, when his turn came, took a piece, and consumed it. Then he felt committed to stay with Father Early until Chicago.

It was some time before Father Early returned to his seat— from making the acquaintance of Monsignor Reed's parishioners. "What we did was split the responsibility. Miss Culhane's in charge of Monsignor's people. Of course, the ultimate responsibility is mine." Peering up the aisle at two middle-aged women drawing water from the cooler, Father Early said, "The one coming this way now," and gazed out the window.

Miss Culhane, a paper cup in each hand, smiled at the Bishop. He smiled back.

When Miss Culhane had passed, Father Early said, "She's been abroad once, and that's more than most of 'em can say. She's a secretary in private life, and it's hard to find a man with much sense of detail. But I don't know . . . From what I've heard already I'd say the good people don't like the idea. I'm afraid they think she stands between them and me."

The other woman, also carrying paper cups, came down the aisle, and again Father Early gazed out the window. So did the Bishop. When the woman had gone by, Father Early commented dryly, "Her friend, whose name escapes me. Between the two of 'em, Bishop . . . Oh, it'll be better for all concerned when Monsignor joins us."

The Bishop knew nothing about this. Reed had told him nothing. "*Monsignor?*"

"Claims he's allergic to trains."

"*Reed?*"

Again Father Early treated the question as rhetorical. "His plane doesn't arrive until noon tomorrow. We sail at four. That doesn't give us much time in New York."

The Bishop was putting it all together. Evidently Reed was planning to have as much privacy as he could on the trip. Seeing his little flock running around loose in the station, though, he must have felt guilty—and then the Bishop had happened along. Would Reed do this to him? Reed had done this to him. Reed had once called the Bishop's diocese the next thing to a titular see.

"I'm sorry he isn't sailing with us," said Father Early.

"Isn't he?"

"He's got business of some kind—stained glass, I believe—that'll keep him in New York for a few days. He may have to go to Boston. So he's flying over. I wonder, Bishop, if he isn't allergic to boats too." Father Early smiled at the Bishop as one good sailor to another.

The Bishop wasn't able to smile back. He was thinking how much he preferred to travel alone. When he was being hustled into the coach by Reed and Father Early, he hadn't considered the embarrassment there might be in the end; together on the train to Chicago and again on the one to New York and then crossing on the same liner, apart, getting an occasional glimpse of each other across the barriers. The perfidious Reed had united them, knowing full well that the Bishop was traveling first class and that Father Early and the group were going tourist. The Bishop hoped there would be time for him to see

Reed in New York. According to Father Early, though, Reed didn't want them to look for him until they saw him. The Bishop wouldn't.

Miss Culhane, in the aisle again, returned with more water. When she passed, the Bishop and Father Early were both looking out the window. "You can't blame 'em," Father Early said. "I wish he'd picked a man for the job. No, they want more than a man, Bishop. They want a priest."

"They've got you," said the Bishop. "And Monsignor will soon be with you."

"Not until we reach Rome."

"*No?*" The Bishop was rocked by this new evidence of Reed's ruthlessness. Father Early and the group were going to Ireland and England first, as the Bishop was, but they'd be spending more time in those countries, about two weeks.

"No," said Father Early. "He won't."

The Bishop got out his breviary. He feared that Father Early would not be easily discouraged. The Bishop, if he could be persuaded to join the group, would more than make up for the loss of Reed. To share the command with such a man as Father Early, however, would be impossible. It would be to serve under him—as Reed may have realized. The Bishop would have to watch out. It would be dangerous for him to offer Father Early plausible excuses, to point out, for instance, that they'd be isolated from each other once they sailed from New York. Such an excuse, regretfully tendered now, could easily commit him to service on this train, and on the next one, and in New York—and the Bishop wasn't at all sure that Father Early wouldn't find a way for him to be with the group aboard ship. The Bishop turned a page.

When Father Early rose and led the pilgrims in the recitation of the rosary, the Bishop put aside his breviary, took out his beads and prayed along with them. After that, Father Early directed the pilgrims in the singing of "Onward, Christian Soldiers"—which was *not* a Protestant hymn, not originally, he said. Monsignor Reed's parishioners didn't know the words, but Father Early got around that difficulty by having everyone sing the notes of the scale, the ladies *la*, the men *do*. The Bishop cursed his luck and wouldn't even pretend to sing. Father Early was in the aisle, beating time with his fist, exhorting some by name to contribute more to the din, clutching others (males) by the shoulders until they did. The Bishop grew afraid that even he might not be exempt, and again sought the protection of his breviary.

He had an early lunch. When he returned to his seat, it was just past noon, and Father Early was waiting in the aisle for him.

"How about a bite to eat, Bishop?"

"I've eaten, Father."

"You eat early, Bishop."

"I couldn't wait."

Father Early did his little ha-ha laugh. "By the way, Bishop, are you planning anything for the time we'll have in Chicago between trains?" Before the Bishop, who was weighing the significance of the question, could reply, Father Early told him that the group was planning a visit to the Art Institute. "The Art Treasures of Vienna are there now."

"I believe I've seen them, Father."

"In Vienna, Bishop?"

"Yes."

"Well, they should be well worth seeing again."

"Yes. But I don't think I'll be seeing them." Not expecting the perfect silence that followed—this from Father Early was more punishing than his talk—the Bishop added, "Not today." Then, after more of that silence, "I've nothing planned,

136

Father." Quickly, not liking the sound of that, "I do have a few things I might do."

Father Early nodded curtly and went away.

The Bishop heard him inviting some of the group to have lunch with him.

During the rest of the afternoon, the indefatigable voice of Father Early came to the Bishop from all over the coach, but the man himself didn't return to his seat. And when the train pulled into the station, Father Early wasn't in the coach. The Bishop guessed he was with the conductor, to whom he had a lot to say, or with the other employees of the railroad, who never seem to be around at the end of a journey. Stepping out of the coach, the Bishop felt like a free man.

Miss Culhane, however, was waiting for him. She introduced him to an elderly couple, the Doyles, who were the only ones in the group not planning to visit the Art Institute. Father Early, she said, understood that the Bishop wasn't planning to do anything in Chicago and would be grateful if the Bishop would keep an eye on the Doyles there. They hadn't been there before.

The Bishop showed them Grant Park from a taxicab, and pointed out the Planetarium, the Aquarium, the Field Museum. "Thought it was the stockyards," Mr. Doyle commented on Soldier Field, giving Mrs. Doyle a laugh. "I'm afraid there isn't time to go there," the Bishop said. He was puzzled by the Doyles. They didn't seem to realize the sight-seeing was for them. He tried them on foot in department stores until he discovered from something Mrs. Doyle said that they were bearing with him. Soon after that they were standing across the street from the Art Institute, with the Bishop asking if they didn't want to cross over and join the group inside. Mr. Doyle said he didn't think they could make it over there alive—a reference to the heavy traffic, serious or not, the Bishop couldn't tell, but offered to take them across. The Doyles could not be tempted. So the three of them wandered around some more, the Doyles usually a step or two behind the Bishop. At last, in the lobby of the Congress Hotel, Mrs. Doyle expressed a desire to sit down. And there they sat, three in a row, in silence, until it was time to take a cab to the station. On the way over, Mr. Doyle, watching the meter, said, "These things could sure cost you."

In the station the Bishop gave the Doyles a gentle shove in the direction of the gate through which some members of the group were passing. A few minutes later, after a visit to the newsstand, he went through the gate unaccompanied. As soon as he entered his Pullman his ears informed him that he'd reckoned without Mr. Hope, the travel agent in Minneapolis. Old pastors wise in the ways of the world and to the escapist urge to which so many of the men, sooner or later, succumbed, thinking it only a love of travel, approved of Mr. Hope's system. If Mr. Hope had a priest going somewhere, he tried to make it a pair; dealt two, he worked for three of a kind; and so on—and nuns, of course, were wild, their presence eminently sobering. All day the Bishop had thought the odds safely against their having accommodations in the same Pullman car, but he found himself next door to Father Early.

They had dinner together. In the Bishop's view, it was fortunate that the young couple seated across the table was resilient from drink. Father Early opened up on the subject of tipping.

"These men," he said, his glance taking in several waiters, and his mouth almost in the ear of the one who was serving them, a cross-looking colored man, "are in a wonderful position to assert their dignity as human beings—which dignity, being from God, may not be sold with impunity. And for a mere pittance at that! Or, what's worse, bought!"

The Bishop, laying down his soup spoon, sat gazing out the window, for which he was again grateful. It was getting dark. The world seen from a train always looked sadder then. Indiana. Ohio next, but he wouldn't see it. Pennsylvania, perhaps, in the early morning, if he didn't sleep well.

"I see what you mean," he heard the young woman saying, "but I just charge it up to expenses."

"Ah, ha," said Father Early. "Then you don't see what I mean."

"Oh, don't I? Well, it's not important. And *please*—don't explain."

The Bishop, coloring, heard nothing from Father Early and thanked God for that. They had been coming to this, or something like it, inevitably they had. And again the Bishop suffered the thought that the couple was associating him with Father Early.

When he had served dessert across the table, the waiter addressed himself to Father Early. "As far as I'm concerned, sir, you're right," he said, and moved off.

The young woman, watching the waiter go, said, "He can't do that to me."

Airily, Father Early was saying, "And this time tomorrow we'll be on our way to Europe."

The Bishop was afraid the conversation would lapse entirely—which might have been the best thing for it in the long run—but the young man was nodding.

"Will this be your first trip?" asked the young woman. She sounded as though she thought it would be.

"My fifth, God willing," Father Early said. "I don't mean that as a commentary on the boat we're taking. Only as a little reminder to myself that we're all of us hanging by a thread here, only a heart's beat from eternity. Which doesn't mean we shouldn't do our best while here. On the contrary. Some people think Catholics oppose progress here below. Look on your garbage can and what do you see? Galvanized. Galvan was a Catholic. Look on your light bulb. Watts. Watt was a Catholic. The Church never harmed Galileo."

Father Early, as if to see how he was doing, turned to the Bishop. The Bishop, however, was dining with his reflection in the window. He had displayed a spark of interest when Father Early began to talk of the trip, believing there was to be a change of subject matter, but Father Early had tricked him.

"And how long in Rome?" asked the young woman.

"Only two days. Some members of the group intend to stay longer, but they won't return with me. Two days doesn't seem long enough, does it? Well, I can't say that I care for Rome. I didn't feel at home there, or anywhere on the Continent. We'll have two good weeks in the British Isles."

"Some people don't travel to feel at home," said the young woman.

To this Father Early replied, "Ireland first and then England. It may interest you to know that about half of the people in the group are carrying the complete works of Shakespeare. I'm hoping the rest of the group will manage to secure copies of the plays and read them before we visit Stratford."

"It sounds like a large order," said the young woman.

"Paperback editions are to be had everywhere," Father Early said with enthusiasm. "By the way, what book would you want if you were shipwrecked on a desert island?"

Apparently the question had novelty for the young man. "That's a hard one," he said.

"Indeed it is. Chesterton, one of the great Catholic writers, said he'd like a manual of shipbuilding, but I don't consider that a serious answer to the question. I'll make it two books because, of course, you'd want the Bible. Some people think

140

Catholics don't read the Bible. But who preserved Scripture in the Dark Ages? Holy monks. Now what do you say? No. Ladies first."

"I think I'd like that book on shipbuilding," said the young woman.

Father Early smiled. "And you, sir?"

"Shakespeare, I guess."

"I was hoping you'd say that."

Then the Bishop heard the young woman inquiring: "Shakespeare wasn't a Catholic, was he?"

The Bishop reached for his glass of water, and saw Father Early observing a moment of down-staring silence. When he spoke his voice was deficient. "As a matter of fact, we don't know. Arguments both ways. But we just don't know. Perhaps it's better that way," he said, and that was all he said. At last he was eating his dinner.

When the young couple rose to leave, the Bishop, who had been waiting for this moment, turned in time to see the young man almost carry out Father Early's strict counsel against tipping. With one look, however, the young woman prevailed over him. The waiter came at once and removed the tip. With difficulty, the Bishop put down the urge to comment. He wanted to say that he believed people should do what they could do, little though it might be, and shouldn't be asked to attempt what was obviously beyond them. The young woman, who probably thought Father Early was just tight, was better off than the young man.

After the waiter came and went again, Father Early sat back and said, "I'm always being surprised by the capacity ordinary people have for sacrifice."

The Bishop swallowed what—again—would have been his comment. Evidently Father Early was forgetting about the young man.

"Thanks for looking after the Doyles. I would've asked you myself but I was in the baggage car. Someone wanted me to say hello to a dog that's going to South Bend. No trouble, were they? What'd you see?"

The Bishop couldn't bring himself to answer either question. "It's hard to know what other people want to do," he said. "They might've had a better guide."

"I can tell you they enjoyed your company, Bishop."

"Oh?" The Bishop, though touched, had a terrible vision of himself doing the capitals of the world with the Doyles.

Father Early handed the Bishop a cigar. "Joe Quirke keeps me well supplied with these," he said, nodding to a beefy middle-aged man two tables away who looked pleased at having caught Father Early's eye. "I believe you know him."

"I met him," the Bishop said, making a distinction. Mr. Quirke had sat down next to him in the club car before dinner, taken up a magazine, put it down after a minute, and offered to buy the Bishop a drink. When the Bishop (who'd been about to order one) refused, Mr. Quirke had apparently taken him for a teetotaler with a past. He said he'd had a little problem until Father Early got hold of him.

Father Early was discussing the youth eating with Mr. Quirke. "Glenn's been in a little trouble at home—and at school. Three schools, I believe. Good family. I have his father's permission to leave him with the Christian Brothers in Ireland, if they'll have him."

When Glenn got up from the table, the Bishop decided he didn't like the look of him. Glenn was short-haired, long-legged, a Doberman pinscher of a boy. He loped out of the diner, followed by Mr. Quirke.

Two problems, thought the Bishop, getting ready to happen —and doubtless there were more of them in the group. Miss Culhane, in her fashion, could make trouble.

142

"There's something I'd like to discuss with you, Bishop."

The Bishop stiffened. Now it was coming, he feared, the all-out attempt to recruit him.

Father Early was looking across the table, at the empty places there. "You realize they'd been drinking?"

The Bishop refused to comment. *Now what?*

"It wouldn't surprise me if they met on this train."

"Yes, well . . ."

"Bishop, in my opinion, the boy is or has been a practicing Catholic."

In the Bishop's opinion, it was none of Father Early's business. He knew what Father Early was getting at, and he didn't like it. Father Early was thinking of taking on more trouble.

"I believe the boy's in danger," Father Early said. "Real danger."

The Bishop opened his mouth to tell Father Early off, but not much came out. "I wouldn't call him a boy." The Bishop felt that Father Early had expected something of the sort from him, nothing, and no support. Father Early had definitely gone into one of his silences. The Bishop, fussing with his cuffs, suddenly reached, but Father Early beat him to the checks.

Father Early complimented the waiter on the service and food, rewarding him with golden words.

The Bishop was going to leave a tip, to be on the safe side, but apparently the waiter was as good as his word. They left the diner in the blaze of his hospitality.

The Bishop had expected to be asked where in New York he'd be saying Mass in the morning, but when they arrived at their doors, Father Early smiled and put out his hand. It certainly looked like good-by.

They shook hands.

And then, suddenly, Father Early was on his knees, his head bowed and waiting for the Bishop's blessing.

His mind was full of the day and he was afraid he was in for one of those nights he'd had on trains before. He kept looking at his watch in the dark, listening for sounds of activity next door, and finally he admitted to himself that he was waiting for Father Early to come in. So he gave Father Early until midnight—and then he got dressed and went out to look for him.

Up ahead he saw Glenn step into the corridor from an end room and go around the corner. The Bishop prepared to say hello. But when he was about to pass, the atmosphere filled up with cigarette smoke. The Bishop hurried through it, unrecognized, he hoped, considering the lateness of the hour and the significance of another visit to the club car, as it might appear to Glenn, who could have observed him there earlier in the evening.

The club car was empty except for a man with a magazine in the middle of the car, the waiter serving him a drink, and the young man and Father Early at the tail end of the train, seated on a sofa facing upon the tracks. The Bishop advanced with difficulty to the rear. The train was traveling too fast.

Father Early glanced around. He moved over on the sofa to make room for the Bishop, and had the young man move. The Bishop sat down beside the young man, who was now in the middle.

"One I went to—we're talking about fairs, Bishop—had an educated donkey, as the fellow called it. This donkey could tell one color from another—knew them all by name. The fellow had these paddles, you've seen them, painted different colors. Red, green, blue, brown, black, orange, yellow, white— oh, all colors . . ."

The Bishop, from the tone of this, sensed that nothing had been resolved and that Father Early's objective was to keep the young man up all night with him. It was a siege.

"The fellow would say, 'Now, Trixie'—I remember the little donkey's name. You might've seen her at some time."

The young man shook his head.

"'Now, Trixie,' the fellow would say, 'bring me the yellow paddle,' and that's what she'd do. She'd go to the rack, where all the paddles were hanging, pick out the yellow one, and carry it to the fellow. Did it with her teeth, of course. Then the fellow would say, 'Trixie, bring me the green paddle.'"

"And she brought the green one," said the young man patiently.

"That's right. The fellow would say, 'Now, Trixie, bring me the paddles that are the colors of the flag.'" Father Early addressed the Bishop: "Red, white, and blue."

"Yes," said the Bishop. What an intricate instrument for good a simple man could be! Perhaps Father Early was only a fool, a ward of heaven, not subject to the usual penalties for meddling. No, it was zeal, and people, however far gone, still expected it from a man of God. But, even so, Father Early ought to be more careful, humbler before the mystery of iniquity. And still . . .

"My, that was a nice little animal, that Trixie." Father Early paused, giving his attention to the signal lights blinking down the tracks, and continued. "Red, green, all colors. Most fairs have little to recommend them. Some fairs, however, are worth while." Father Early stood up. "I'll be right back," he said, and went to the lavatory.

The Bishop was about to say something—to keep the ball rolling—when the young man got up and left, without a word.

The Bishop sat where he was until he heard the lavatory door open and shut. Then he got up to meet Father Early. Father Early looked beyond the Bishop, toward the place where the young man had been, and then at the Bishop. He didn't appear to blame the Bishop at all. Nothing was said.

They walked in the direction from which Father Early had just come. The Bishop thought they were calling it a day, but Father Early was onto something else, trying the waiter on baseball.

"Good night, Father."

"Oh?" said Father Early, as if he'd expected the Bishop to stick around for it.

"Good night, Father." The Bishop had a feeling that baseball wouldn't last, that the sermon on tipping was due again.

"Good night, Bishop."

The Bishop moved off comically, as the train made up for lost time. Entering his Pullman car, he saw the young man, who must have been kept waiting, disappear into the room Glenn had come out of earlier.

The Bishop slept well that night, after all, but not before he thought of Father Early still out there, on his feet and trying, which was what counted in the sight of God, not success. *Thinkest thou that I cannot ask my Father, and he will give me presently more than twelve legions of angels?*

"Would you like me to run through these names with you, Bishop, or do you want to familiarize yourself with the people as we go along?"

"I'd prefer that, I think. And I wish you'd keep the list, Miss Culhane."

"I don't think Father Early would want you to be without it, Bishop."

"No? Very well, I'll keep it then."

BLUE ISLAND

On the day the Daviccis moved into their house, Ethel was
visited by a Welcome Wagon hostess bearing small gifts from
local merchants, but after that by nobody for three weeks,
only Ralph's relatives and door-to-door salesmen. And then
Mrs. Hancock came smiling. They sat on the matching green
chairs which glinted with threads of what appeared to be
gold. In the picture window, the overstimulated plants grew
wild in pots.

Mrs. Hancock had guessed right about Ethel and Ralph,
that they were newlyweds. "Am I right in thinking you're of
Swedish descent, Mrs. Davicky? You, I mean?"

Ethel smiled, as if taking a compliment, and said nothing.

"I only ask because so many people in the neighborhood
are. I'm not, myself," said Mrs. Hancock. She was unnaturally
pink, with tinted blue hair. Her own sharp-looking teeth were
transparent at the tips. "But you're so fair."

"My maiden name was Taylor," Ethel said. It was, and it
wasn't—it was the name she'd got at the orphanage. Wanting
a cigarette, she pushed the silver box on the coffee table
toward Mrs. Hancock.

Mrs. Hancock used one of her purple claws to pry up the

147

first cigarette from the top layer. "A good old American name like mine."

She was making too much of it, Ethel thought, and wondered about Mrs. Hancock's maiden name.

"Is your husband in business, Mrs. Davicky?"

"Yes, he is." Ethel put the lighter—a simple column of silver, the mate to the box—to Mrs. Hancock's cigarette and then to her own.

"Not here in Blue Island?"

"No." From here on, it could be difficult. Ralph was afraid that people in the neighborhood would disapprove of his business. "In Minneapolis." The Mohawk Inn, where Ethel had worked as a waitress, was first-class—thick steaks, dark lights, an electric organ—but Ralph's other places, for which his brothers were listed as the owners, were cut-rate bars on or near Washington Avenue. "He's a distributor," Ethel said, heading her off. "Non-alcoholic beverages mostly." It was true. Ralph had taken over his family's wholesale wine business, never much in Minneapolis, and got it to pay by converting to soft drinks.

Mrs. Hancock was noticing the two paintings which, because of their size and the lowness of the ceiling, hung two feet from the floor, but she didn't comment on them. "Lovely, lovely," she said, referring to the driftwood lamp in the picture window. A faraway noise came from her stomach. She raised her voice. "But you've been lonely, haven't you? I could see it when I came in. It's this neighborhood."

"It's very nice," said Ethel quickly. Maybe Mrs. Hancock was at war with the neighbors, looking for an ally.

"I suppose you know Mrs. Nilgren," said Mrs. Hancock, nodding to the left.

"No, but I've seen her. Once she waved."

"She's nice. Tied down with children, though." Mrs. Hancock nodded to the right. "How about old Mrs. Mann?"

"I don't think anybody's there now."

"The Manns are away! California. So you don't know anybody yet?"

"No."

"I'm surprised you haven't met some of them at the Cashway."

"I never go there," Ethel said. "Ralph—that's my husband—he wants me to trade at the home-owned stores."

"Oh?" Mrs. Hancock's stomach cut loose again. "I didn't know people still felt that way." Mrs. Hancock looked down the street, in the direction of the little corner store. "Do they do much business?"

"No," said Ethel. The old couple who ran it were suspicious of her, she thought, for buying so much from them. The worst of it was that Ralph had told her to open a charge account, and she hadn't, and she never knew when he'd stop there and try to use it. There was a sign up in the store that said: In God We Trust—All Others Pay Cash.

"I'll bet that's it," Mrs. Hancock was saying. "I'm afraid people are pretty clannish around here—and the Wagners have so many friends. They live one-two-three-five houses down." Mrs. Hancock had been counting the houses across the street. "Mr. Wagner's the manager of the Cashway."

Ethel was holding her breath.

"I'm afraid so," said Mrs. Hancock.

Ethel sighed. It was Ralph's fault. She'd always wanted to trade at the Cashway.

Mrs. Hancock threw back her head, inhaling, and her eyelids, like a doll's, came down. "I'm afraid it's your move, Mrs. Davicky."

Ethel didn't feel that it was her move at all and must have shown it.

149

Mrs. Hancock sounded impatient. "Invite 'em in. Have 'em in for a morning coffee."

"I couldn't do that," Ethel said. "I've never been to a coffee." She'd only read about coffees in the women's magazines to which Ralph had subscribed for her. "I wouldn't know what to do."

"Nothing to it. Rolls, coffee, and come as you are. Of course nobody really does, not really." Mrs. Hancock's stomach began again. "Oh, shut up," she said to it. "I've just come from one too many." Mrs. Hancock made a face, showing Ethel a brown mohair tongue. She laughed at Ethel. "Cheer up. It wasn't in this neighborhood."

Ethel felt better. "I'll certainly think about it," she said.

Mrs. Hancock rose, smiling, and went over to the telephone. "You'll do it right now," she said, as though being an older woman entitled her to talk that way to Ethel. "They're probably dying to get inside this lovely house."

After a moment, Ethel, who was already on her feet, having thought that Mrs. Hancock was leaving, went over and sat down to telephone. In the wall mirror she saw how she must appear to Mrs. Hancock. When the doorbell had rung, she'd been in too much of a hurry to see who it was to do anything about her lips and hair. "Will they know who I am?"

"Of course." Mrs. Hancock squatted on the white leather hassock with the phone book. "And you don't have to say I'm coming. Oh, I'll come. I'll be more than happy to. You don't need me, though. All you need is confidence."

And Mrs. Hancock was right. Ethel called eight neighbors, and six could come on Wednesday morning, which Mrs. Hancock had thought would be the best time for her. Two of the six even sounded anxious to meet Ethel, and, surprisingly, Mrs. Wagner was one of these.

"You did it all yourself," said Mrs. Hancock.

"With your help," said Ethel, feeling indebted to Mrs. Hancock, intimately so. It was as if they'd cleaned the house together.

They were saying good-by on the front stoop when Ralph rolled into the driveway. Ordinarily at noon he parked just outside the garage, but that day he drove in—without acknowledging them in any way. "Mr. Daveechee," Ethel commented. For Mrs. Hancock, after listening to Ethel pronounce her name for all the neighbors, was still saying "Davicky."

Mrs. Hancock stayed long enough to get the idea that Ralph wasn't going to show himself. She went down the front walk saying, " 'Bye now."

While Mrs. Hancock was getting into her car, which seemed a little old for the neighborhood, Ralph came out of the garage.

Mrs. Hancock waved and nodded—which, Ethel guessed, was for Ralph's benefit, the best Mrs. Hancock could do to introduce herself at the distance. She drove off. Too late, Ralph's hand moved up to wave. He stared after Mrs. Hancock's moving car with a look that just didn't belong to him, Ethel thought, a look that she hadn't seen on his face until they moved out to Blue Island.

During lunch, Ethel tried to reproduce her conversation with Mrs. Hancock, but she couldn't tell Ralph enough. He wanted to know the neighbors' names, and she could recall the names of only three. Mrs. Wagner, one of them, was very popular in the neighborhood, and her husband . . .

"You go to the Cashway then. Some of 'em sounded all right, huh?"

"Ralph, they all sounded all right, real friendly. The man next door sells insurance. Mr. Nilgren."

Ethel remembered that one of the husbands was a lawyer and told Ralph that. He left the table. A few minutes later Ethel heard him driving away.

It had been a mistake to mention the lawyer to Ralph. It had made him think of the shooting they'd had at the Bow Wow, one of the joints. There had been a mix-up, and Ralph's home address had appeared in the back pages of one of the papers when the shooting was no longer news. Ethel doubted that the neighbors had seen the little item. Ralph might be right about the lawyer, though, who would probably have to keep up with everything like that.

Ralph wouldn't have worried so much about such a little thing in the old days. He was different now. It was hard to get him to smile. Ethel could remember how he would damn the Swedes for slapping higher and higher taxes on liquor and to-bacco, but now, when she pointed out a letter some joker had written to the paper suggesting a tax on coffee, or when she showed him the picture of the wife of the Minnesota senator —the fearless one—christening an ore boat with a bottle of milk, which certainly should've given Ralph a laugh, he was silent.

It just made Ethel sick to see him at the windows, watching Mr. Nilgren, a sandy-haired, dim-looking man who wore plaid shirts and a red cap in the yard. Mr. Nilgren would be raking out his hedge, or wiring up the skinny little trees, or washing his car if it was Sunday morning, and there Ralph would be, behind a drape. One warm day Ethel had seen Mr. Nilgren in the yard with a golf club, and had said, "He should get some of those little balls that don't go anywhere." It had been pain-ful to see Ralph then. She could almost *hear* him thinking. He would get some of those balls and give them to Mr. Nilgren as a present. No, it would look funny if he did. Then he got that sick look that seemed to come from wanting to do a favor for someone who might not let him do it.

A couple of days later Ethel learned that Ralph had gone to an indoor driving range to take golf lessons. He came home happy, with a club he was supposed to swing in his spare time. He'd made a friend, too, another beginner. They were going to have the same schedule and be measured for clubs. During his second lesson, however, he quit. Ethel wasn't surprised, for Ralph, though strong, was awkward. She was better than he was with a hammer and nails, and he mutilated the heads of screws. When he went back the second time, it must have been too much for him, finding out he wasn't any better, after carrying the club around the house for three days. Ethel asked about the other beginner, and at first Ralph acted as though she'd made him up, and then he hotly rejected the word "friend," which she'd used. Finally he said, "If you ask me, that bastard's played before!"

That was just like him. At the coffee, Ethel planned to ask the women to come over soon with their husbands, but she was afraid some of the husbands wouldn't take to Ralph. Probably he could buy insurance from Mr. Nilgren. He would want to do something for the ones who weren't selling anything, though—if there were any like that—and they might misunderstand Ralph. He was used to buying the drinks. He should relax and take the neighbors as they came. Or move.

She didn't know why they were there anyway. It was funny. After they were married, before they left on their honeymoon, Ralph had driven her out to Blue Island and walked her through the house. That was all there was to it. Sometimes she wondered if he'd won the house at cards. She didn't know why they were there when they could just as well be living at Minnetonka or White Bear, where they could keep a launch like the one they'd hired in Florida—and where the houses were far apart and neighbors wouldn't matter so much. What were they waiting for? Some of the things they owned, she knew, were for later. They didn't need sterling for eighteen in Blue Island. And the two big pictures were definitely for later.

She didn't know what Ralph liked about his picture, which was of an Indian who looked all in sitting on a horse that looked all in, but he had gone to the trouble of ordering it from a regular art store. Hers was more cheerful, the palace of the Doge of Venice, Italy. Ralph hadn't wanted her to have it at first. He was really down on anything foreign. (There were never any Italian dishes on the menu at the Mohawk.) But she believed he liked her for wanting that picture, for having a weakness for things Italian, for him—and even for his father and mother, whom he was always sorry to see and hadn't invited to the house. When they came anyway, with his brothers, their wives and children (and wine, which Ralph wouldn't touch), Ralph was in and out, upstairs and down, never long in the same room with them, never encouraging them to stay when they started to leave. They called him "Rock" or "Rocky," but Ralph didn't always answer to that. To one of the little boys who had followed him down into the basement, Ethel had heard him growl, "The name's Ralph"—that to a nine-year-old. His family must have noticed the change in Ralph, but they were wrong if they blamed her, just because she was a little young for him, a blonde, and not a Catholic—not that Ralph went to church. In fact, she thought Ralph would be better off with his family for his friends, instead of counting so much on the neighbors. She liked Ralph's family and enjoyed having them in the house.

And if Ralph's family hadn't come around, the neighbors might even think they weren't properly married, that they had a love nest going there. Ethel didn't blame the neighbors for being suspicious of her and Ralph. Mr. Nilgren in his shirt and cap that did nothing for him, he belonged there, but not Ralph, so dark, with his dark blue suits, pearl-gray hats, white jacquard shirts—and with her, with her looks and platinum hair. She tried to dress down, to look like an older woman, when she went out. The biggest thing in their favor, but it wasn't noticeable yet, was the fact that she was pregnant.

Sometimes she thought Ralph must be worrying about the baby—as she was—about the kind of life a little kid would have in a neighborhood where his father and mother didn't know anybody. There were two pre-school children at the Nilgrens'. Would they play with the Davicci kid? Ethel didn't ever want to see that sick look of Ralph's on a child of hers.

That afternoon two men in white overalls arrived from Minneapolis in a white truck and washed the windows inside and out, including the basement and garage. Ralph had sent them. Ethel sat in the dining room and polished silver to the music of *Carmen* on records. She played whole operas when Ralph wasn't home.

In bed that night Ralph made her run through the neighbors again. Seven for sure, counting Mrs. Hancock. "Is that all?" Ethel said she was going to call the neighbor who hadn't been home. "When?" When she got the number from Mrs. Hancock. "When's that?" When Mrs. Hancock phoned, if she phoned . . . And that was where Ralph believed Ethel had really fallen down. She didn't have Mrs. Hancock's number—or address—and there wasn't a Hancock listed for Blue Island in the phone book. "How about next door?" Mrs. Nilgren was still coming. "The other side?" The Manns were still away, in California, and Ralph knew it. "They might come back. Ever think of that? You don't wanna leave them out." *Them,* he'd said, showing Ethel what was expected of her. He wanted those husbands. Ethel promised to watch for the return of the Manns. "They could come home in the night." Ethel reminded Ralph that a person in her condition needed a lot of sleep, and Ralph left her alone then.

Before Ralph was up the next morning, Ethel started to

clean the house. Ralph was afraid the house cleaning wouldn't be done right (*he* spoke of her condition) and wanted to get another crew of professionals out from Minneapolis. Ethel said it wouldn't look good. She said the neighbors expected them to do their own house cleaning—*and window washing*. Ralph shut up.

When he came home for lunch, Ethel was able to say that Mrs. Hancock had called and that the neighbor who hadn't been home could come to the coffee. Ethel had talked to her, and she had sounded very friendly. "That's three of 'em, huh?" Ethel was tired of that one, but told him they'd *all* sounded friendly to her. "Mrs. Hancock okay?" Mrs. Hancock was okay. More than happy to be coming. Ralph asked if Ethel had got Mrs. Hancock's phone number and address. No. "Why not?" Mrs. Hancock would be there in the morning. That was why— and Ralph should get a hold on himself.

In the afternoon, after he was gone, Ethel put on one of her new conservative dresses and took the bus to Minneapolis to buy some Swedish pastry. She wanted something better than she could buy in Blue Island. In the window of the store where they'd bought Ralph's Indian, there were some little miniatures, lovely New England snow scenes. She hesitated to go in when she saw the sissy clerk was on duty again. He had made Ralph sore, asking how he'd like to have the Indian framed in birch bark. The Mohawk was plastered with birch bark, and Ralph thought the sissy recognized him and was try- ing to be funny. "This is going into my home!" Ralph had said, and ordered the gold frame costing six times as much as the Indian. However, he'd taken the sissy's advice about having a light put on it. Ethel hesitated, but she went in. In his way, the sissy was very nice, and Ethel went home with five little Old English prints. When she'd asked about the pictures in the window, the New England ones, calling them "landscapes," he'd said "snowscapes" and looked disgusted, as if they weren't what she should want.

When she got home, she hung the prints over the sofa where there was a blank space, and they looked fine in their shiny black frames. She didn't say anything to Ralph, hoping he'd notice them, but he didn't until after supper. "Hey, what *is* this?" he said. He bounced off the sofa, confronting her.

"Ralph, they're cute!"

"Not in my home!"

"Ralph, they're humorous!" The clerk had called them that. Ralph called them drunks and whores. He had Ethel feeling ashamed of herself. It was hard to believe that she could have felt they were just fat and funny and just what their living room needed, as the clerk had said. Ralph took them down. "Man or woman sell 'em to you?" Ethel, seeing what he had in mind, knew she couldn't tell him where she'd got them. She lied. "I was in Dayton's . . ."

"A woman—all right, then *you* can take 'em back!"

She was scared. Something like that was enough to make Ralph regret *marrying* her—and to remind her again that she couldn't have made him. If there had been a showdown between them, he would've learned about her first pregnancy. It would've been easy for a lawyer to find out about that. She'd listened to an old doctor who'd told her to go ahead and have it, that she'd love her little baby, who hadn't lived, but there would be a record anyway. She wasn't sorry about going to a regular hospital to have it, though it made it harder for her now, having that record. She'd done what she could for the baby. She hated to think of the whole thing, but when she did, as she did that evening, she knew she'd done her best.

It might have been a bad evening for her, with Ralph brooding on her faults, if a boy hadn't come to the door selling chances on a raffle. Ralph bought all the boy had, over five dollars' worth, and asked where he lived in the neighborhood. "I live in Minneapolis."

"Huh? Whatcha doin' way out here then?" The boy said it was easier to sell chances out there. Ethel, who had been doing the dishes, returned to the sink before Ralph could see her. He went back to his *Reader's Digest*, and she slipped off to bed, early, hoping his mind would be occupied with the boy if she kept out of sight.

He came to bed after the ten o'clock news. "You awake?" Ethel, awake, but afraid he wanted to talk neighbors, moaned remotely. "If anybody comes to the door sellin' anything, make sure it's somebody local."

In the morning, Ralph checked over the silver and china laid out in the dining room and worried over the pastry. "Fresh?" Fresh! She'd put it in the deep freeze right away and it hadn't even thawed out yet. "Is that *all?*" That was all, and it was more than enough. She certainly didn't need a whole quart of whipping cream. "Want me to call up for something to go with this?" No. "Turkey or a ham? I maybe got time to go myself if I go right now." He carried on like that until ten o'clock, when she got rid of him, saying, "You wouldn't want to be the only man, Ralph."

Then she was on her own, wishing Mrs. Hancock would come early and see her through the first minutes.

But Mrs. Wagner was the first to arrive. After that, the neighbors seemed to ring the bell at regular intervals. Ethel met them at the door, hung their coats in the hall closet, returning each time to Mrs. Wagner in the kitchen. They were all very nice, but Mrs. Wagner was the nicest.

"Now let's just let everything be," she said after they'd arranged the food in the dining room. "Let's go in and meet your friends."

They found the neighbors standing before the two pictures. Ethel snapped on the spotlights. She heard little cries of pleasure all around.

"Heirlooms!"

"Is Mr. Davitchy a collector?"

"Just likes good things, huh?"

"I just love this lamp."

"I just *stare* at it when I go by."

"So do I."

Ethel, looking at her driftwood lamp, her plants, and beyond, stood in a haze of pleasure. Earlier, when she was giving her attention to Mrs. Nilgren (who was telling about the trouble "Carl" had with his trees), Ethel had seen Ralph's car cruise by, she thought, and now again, but this time there was no doubt of it. She recognized the rather old one parked in front as Mrs. Hancock's, but where was Mrs. Hancock?

"Hello, everybody!"

Mrs. Hancock had let herself in, and was hanging up her coat.

Ethel disappeared into the kitchen. She carried the coffeepot, which had been on *low,* into the dining room, where they were supposed to come and help themselves. She stood by the pot, nervous, ready to pour, hoping that someone would look in and see that she was ready, but no one did.

She went to see what they were doing. They were still sitting down, listening to Mrs. Hancock. She'd had trouble with her car. That was why she was late. She saw Ethel. "I can see you want to get started," she said, rising. "So do I."

Ethel returned to the dining room and stood by the coffeepot.

Mrs. Hancock came first. "Starved," she said. She carried off her coffee, roll, and two of the little Swedish cookies, and Ethel heard her in the living room rallying the others.

They came then, quietly, and Ethel poured. When all had been served, she started another pot of coffee, and took her cup and a cookie—she wasn't hungry—into the living room.

Mrs. Hancock, sitting on the hassock, had a bottle in her hand. On the rug around her were some brushes and one copper pan. "Ladies," she was saying, "now here's something new." Noticing Ethel, Mrs. Hancock picked up the pan. "How'd you like to have this for your kitchen? Here."

Ethel crossed the room. She carried the pan back to where she'd been standing.

"This is no ordinary polish," continued Mrs. Hancock, shaking the bottle vigorously. "This is what is known as liquefied ointment. It possesses rare medicinal properties. It renews wood. It gives you a base for polishing—something to shine that simply wasn't there before. There's nothing like it on the market—not in the polish field. It's a Shipshape product, and you all know what that means." Mrs. Hancock opened the bottle and dabbed at the air. "Note the handy applicator." Snatching a cloth from her lap, she rubbed the leg of the coffee table—"remove all foreign matter first"—and dabbed at the leg with the applicator. "This does for wood what liniment does for horses. It relaxes the grain, injects new life, *soothes* the wood. Well, how do you like it?" she called over to Ethel.

Ethel glanced down at the pan, forgotten in her hand.

"Pass it around," said Mrs. Hancock.

Ethel offered the pan to Mrs. Nilgren, who was nearest.

"I've seen it, thanks."

Ethel moved to the next neighbor.

"I've seen it."

Ethel moved on. "Mrs. Wagner, have you?"

"Many times"—with a smile.

Ethel looked back where she'd been standing before she started out with the pan—and went the other way, finally stepping into the hallway. There she saw a canvas duffel bag on the side of which was embossed a pennant flying the word SHIPSHAPE. And hearing Mrs. Hancock—"And this is new, girls. Can you all see from where you're sitting?"—Ethel began to move again. She kept right on going.

Upstairs, in the bedroom, lying down, she noticed the pan in her hand. She shook it off. It hit the headboard of the bed, denting the traditional mahogany, and came to rest in the satin furrow between Ralph's pillow and hers. Oh, God! In a minute, she'd have to get up and go down to them and do *something*— but then she heard the coat hangers banging back empty in the closet downstairs, and the front door opening and, finally, closing. There was a moment of perfect silence in the house before her sudden sob, then another moment before she heard someone coming, climbing the carpeted stairs.

Ethel foolishly thought it would be Mrs. Wagner, but of course it was Mrs. Hancock, after her pan.

She tiptoed into the room, adjusted the venetian blind, and seated herself lightly on the edge of the bed. "Don't think I don't know how you feel," she said. "Not that it shows yet. I wasn't *sure*, dear." She looked into Ethel's eyes, frightening her.

As though only changing positions, Ethel moved the hand that Mrs. Hancock was after.

"My ointment would fix that, restore the surface," said Mrs. Hancock, her finger searching the little wound in the headboard. She began to explain, gently—like someone with a terrible temper warming up: "When we first started having these little Shipshape parties, they didn't tell each other. They do now, oh, yes, or they would if I'd let them. I'm on to them. They're just in it for the mops now. You get one, you know, for having the party in your home. It's collapsible, ideal for the small home or travel. But the truth is you let me down! Why, when you left the room the way you did, you didn't give them any choice. Why, I don't think there's one of that crowd—with the exception of May Wagner—that isn't using one of my free mops! Why, they just walked out on me!"

Ethel, closing her eyes, saw Mrs. Hancock alone, on the hassock, with her products all around her.

"It's a lot of pan for the money," Mrs. Hancock was saying now. She reached over Ethel's body for it. "You'll love your little pan," she said, fondling it.

Ethel's eyes were resisting Mrs. Hancock, but her right hand betrayed her.

"Here?" Mrs. Hancock opened a drawer, took out a purse, and handed it over, saying, "Only $12.95."

Ethel found a five and a ten.

"You *do* want the ointment, don't you? The pan and the large bottle come to a little more than this, but it's not enough to worry about."

Mrs. Hancock got up, apparently to leave.

Ethel thought of something. "You do live in Blue Island, don't you?" Ralph would be sure to ask about that—if she had to tell him. And she would!

"Not any more, thank God."

Ethel nodded. She wasn't surprised.

Mrs. Hancock, at the door, peeked out—reminding Ethel of a bored visitor looking for a nurse who would tell her it was time to leave the patient. "You'll find your ointment and mop downstairs," she said. "I just know everything's going to be all right." Then she smiled and left.

When, toward noon, Ethel heard Ralph come into the driveway, she got out of bed, straightened the spread, and concealed the pan in the closet. She went to the window and gazed down upon the crown of his pearl-gray hat. He was carrying a big club of roses.

162

THE PRESENCE OF GRACE

On a fine Sunday morning in June, Father Fabre opened the announcement book to familiarize himself with the names of the deceased in the parish for whom Masses would be offered in the coming week, and came upon a letter from the chancery office. The letter, dated December, dealt with the Legion of Decency pledge which should have been administered to the people at that time. Evidently Father Fabre was supposed to read it at the nine-thirty and eleven o'clock Masses that morning. He went to look for the pastor.

Father Fabre, ordained not quite a year, had his hands full at Trinity. It wasn't a well-run parish. The pastor was a hard man to interest in a problem. They saw each other at meals. Father Fabre had been inside the pastor's bedroom, the seat of all his inactivity, only once; Miss Burke, the housekeeper, never. The press of things was very great in the pastor's room, statues, candlesticks, cases of sacramental wine, bales of pious literature and outdated collection envelopes, two stray pews and a prie-dieu, the implements and furniture of his calling. There was a large table-model radio in his bed, and he obviously slept and made the bed around it. That was about it.

Father Fabre found the pastor in the dining room. "Little

late for this, isn't it?" he said. He held out the letter which had
wintered in the pastor's room.

"Don't watch me eat," said the pastor, a graying dormouse.
He had had the six-thirty and eight o'clocks, and was breaking
his fast—not very well, Father Fabre thought, still trying to see
what was in the bowl. Shredded wheat *and* oatmeal? Something he'd made himself? Not necessarily. Miss Burke could
make dishes like that.

The pastor shifted into a sidesaddle position, bending one of
his narrow shoulders over the bowl, obstructing the curate's
view.

Father Fabre considered the letter in his hand. . . . *im-
moral motion pictures / demoralizing television / indecent
plays / vulgar radio programs / pernicious books / vicious
papers and periodicals / degrading dance halls / and un-
wholesome taverns* . . . Was this the mind, the tongue of
the Church? "Little late for this, isn't it?"

"No."

"I thought we were supposed to give it a long time ago." On
the Sunday within the Octave of the Immaculate Conception,
in fact. On that day, Trinity, pledgeless, had been unique
among the churches of the diocese—so he'd bragged to friends,
curates who were unhappy about the pledge, as he was, and
he hadn't really blamed them for what they'd said out of envy,
that it had been his duty to repair the omission at his Masses.
"Weren't we?"

"No."

"*No?*"

The dormouse shook his head a half inch. The spoon in his
right hand was a precision instrument, scraping up the last of
whatever had filled the bowl. Grain.

"I don't feel right about this," Father Fabre said, going away
with the letter. He went to the sacristy to vest for the nine-

thirty, talking to himself. It *was* a little late for the pledge. *No.*
The Sunday within the Octave *had* been the day for it. *No.*

The white fiddleback chasuble he was putting on had been
spoiled on Christmas. He'd been vesting, as now, when the
pastor, writing out a Mass card for a parishioner, had flicked
his pen at the floor to get the ink flowing. Father Fabre had
called his attention to the ink spots on the chasuble. " 'S not
ink," he'd said. Asked what it was, he'd said, " 'S not ink," and
that was all he'd say. For a time, after that, Father Fabre wondered if the pastor's pen could contain some new kind of writing fluid—not ink—and thought perhaps the spots would disappear. The spots, the *'s not ink* spots, were still there. But
a recent incident seemed to explain the pastor's odd denials.
"Not a ball point, is it?" he'd said to Father Fabre, who was
about to fill his fountain pen from the big bottle in the office.
"*No,* Father," said Father Fabre, presenting his pen for inspec-
tion. "Takes ink," said the pastor. "*Yes,* Father." The pastor
pointed to the big bottle from which Father Fabre customarily
filled his pen, and said, "Why don't you try that?" "Say, that's
an idea," said Father Fabre, going the pastor one better. "Better go and flush your pen with water first," said the pastor.
And the funny part was that Father Fabre had gone and
flushed his pen before filling it from the big bottle that time.
"I think you'll like *that,*" said the pastor. *That* was *Quink.* The
dormouse had the casuist's gift, and more.

He escaped much of man's fate. Instead of arguing his way
out of a jam, or confessing himself in error, the pastor simply
denied everything. It was simple—as simple as when he, as
priest, changed the bread and wine into the body and blood of
Christ. But he had no power from his priesthood to deny the
undeniable, for instance that he'd spoiled a good chasuble.
When he said " 'S not ink," nothing was changed. He could

really slow you up, though, if you were inclined to disagree with him and to be rational about it.

When the pastor entered the sacristy before the nine-thirty, Father Fabre was ready for him. "Father," he said, "I can't give this pledge in conscience—not as it's given in some parishes. I can't ask the people to rise as a body and raise their right hands, to repeat after me words which many of them either don't understand the full meaning of, or don't mean to abide by. I don't see anything *wrong* with giving it to those who mean to keep it." He'd wrangled against the pledge in the seminary. If it was "not an oath," as some maintained, wasn't it administered by a priest in church, and didn't it cheapen the clergy to participate in such a ceremony, and one which many merely paid lip service to? Didn't the chancery use the word "invite" and wasn't "demand" the word for the way the thing was rammed through in some parishes? Couldn't outsiders, with some justice, call the whole procedure totalitarian? What *did* Rome think of it? Wasn't it a concession to the rather *different* tone in America, a pacifier?

But the pastor had gone, saying, "Just so you give it."

Father Fabre got behind his servers and started them moving toward the altar. He saw the pastor in front of a battery of vigil lights, picking up the burned matches. Parishioners who had used them would be surprised to know that the pastor blew out all the lights after the last Mass. "Fire hazard," he'd said, caught in the act.

Before the eleven o'clock, after resting a few minutes between Masses in his room, he went to the bathroom and called down the laundry chute to Miss Burke in the kitchen. "Don't set a place for me. I'm invited out for dinner." He stood ready at the chute to cut her off but heard only a sigh and something about the pastor having said the same thing. He hadn't expected to get away with it so easily. They were having another critical period, and it was necessary, as before, to stand up to her. "I hope I let you know soon enough," he said. She should be happy, with them both gone. She wouldn't have to cook at all. And he was doing her the honor of pretending that she planned their meals ahead.

"Father!"

"Yes, Miss Burke."

"Is it Mrs. Mathers' you're going to?"

He delayed his reply in the hope that she'd see the impertinence of the question, and when this should have been accomplished, he said, "I hope I let you know in time."

He heard the little door slam at the other end of the chute. Then, as always in time of stress, she was speaking intimately to friendly spirits who, of course, weren't there, and then wailing like the wind. "Sure she was puttin' it around she'd have him over! But we none of us"—by which Father Fabre assumed she meant the Altar and Rosary Society—"thought he'd go *there!* Oh, Lord!"

He'd lost the first fall to the pastor, but he'd thrown Miss Burke.

Going downstairs, he heard the coin machines start up in the pastor's room, the tambourines of the separator, the castanets of the counter. The pastor was getting an early start on the day's collections. He wore a green visor in his room and worked under fluorescent tubes. Sometimes he worked a night shift. It was like a war plant, his room, except that no help was wanted. The pastor lived to himself, in a half-light.

In the hallway downstairs, John, the janitor, sitting in the umbrella chair, was having coffee. The chair had a looking-glass back, and when John turned his head he appeared to have two faces.

"Thought you had the day off," said Father Fabre.

"Always plenty to do around here, Father."

"I suppose." They knew each other well enough now for John not to get off that old one about wanting to spend the day with his family.

"She's really rarin' in there," John said. "I had to come out here." He glanced down at the floor, at the cup of muddy water cooling there, and then fearfully in the direction of the kitchen. This did not impress Father Fabre, however, who believed that the janitor and the housekeeper lived in peace. "Not her responsibility," John said.

Father Fabre, knowing he was being tempted, would not discuss the housekeeper with the janitor. Curates came and went, and even pastors, but the janitor, a subtle Slav, stayed on at Trinity.

"I told her it was none of her business."

"*What* isn't?"

"If you want to go there, that's your business," John said. "I had to come out here." John reached down for his cup, without looking, because his hand knew right where it was. "I don't blame you for being sore at her, Father." ("I'm not," Father Fabre murmured, but John, drinking, smiled into his cup.) "I told her it's your business what you do. 'He's old enough,' I said."

"What's she got against Mrs. Mathers?" Father Fabre asked, wondering if Mrs. Mathers was any match for the housekeeper. A natural leader vs. a mental case. It might be close if the Altar and Rosary Society took sides. But the chances were that Miss Burke would soon be fighting on another front. Impossible for her to wage as many wars as she declared.

"Hell, you know how these old maids are, Father," John was saying. "Just needs a man. *You* can understand that."

Father Fabre, calling it a draw with John, turned away and left.

The other guests at Mrs. Mathers' didn't act like Catholics. Mr. Pint, a small man in his sixties, was surprisingly unfriendly, and his daughter, though rather the opposite, went at Father Fabre the wrong way. It might have been the absence of excess respect in her manner that he found unsettling. But Mrs. Mathers, a large motherly but childless widow with puffy elbows, had baked a cake, and was easy to take.

They were all on the back porch of her second floor flat, watching Mr. Pint make ice cream.

"Let me taste it, Dad," Velma said.

"I can't be standin' here all day with this cream gettin' soft on me," Mr. Pint said.

Velma pouted. She had on a purple dress which reminded Father Fabre of the purple veils they'd had on the statues in church during Passiontide. Otherwise there was nothing lenten about Velma, he thought.

"If you taste it now," he said, "it'll just take that much longer to harden."

Mr. Pint, who might have agreed with that, said nothing. He dropped a handful of rock salt into the freezer, a wood-and-iron affair that must have been as old as he was, and sank again to his knees. He resumed cranking.

Father Fabre smiled at Mrs. Mathers. Parishioners expected a priest to be nice and jolly, and that was how he meant to be at Mrs. Mathers'. With Mr. Pint setting the tone, it might not be easy. Father Fabre hadn't expected to be the second most important person there. The cake, he believed, had not been baked for him.

"Your good suit," said Mrs. Mathers. She snatched a *Better Homes and Gardens* from a pile of such magazines and slid it under Mr. Pint's knees.

"Sir Walter Reilly," said Velma, looking at Father Fabre to see if he followed her.

He nodded, doubting her intelligence, wondering if she was bright enough to be a nurse. Mrs. Mathers was a registered nurse.

"Aw, come on," Velma said. "Let me taste it, Dad."

Mr. Pint churned up a chunk of ice and batted it down with the heel of his hand. "By Dad!" he breathed, a little god invoking himself.

Mrs. Mathers wisely retired to the kitchen. Velma, after a moment, ingloriously followed.

Father Fabre gazed over the porch railing. With all the apartment buildings backed up together, it was like a crowded harbor, but with no sign of life—a port of plague. Miss Burke, he remembered, had warned him not to go. John, however, had said go. Mr. Pint's shirt had broken out in patches of deeper blue, and his elastic suspenders, of soft canary hue, were stained a little. Pity moved Father Fabre to offer the helping hand, prudence stayed it, then pity rose again. "Let me take it awhile," he said quietly.

But Mr. Pint, out to deny his size and years, needed no help, or lost in his exertions, had not heard.

Father Fabre went inside, where he found the women, by contrast, laughing and gay. Velma left off tossing the salad, and Mrs. Mathers' stirring spoon hung expectantly in mid-air. "I'm afraid I wasn't much help out there," he said.

"That's just Dad's way," Mrs. Mathers said. "Come in here a minute, Father, if you want to see something nice."

Mrs. Mathers led him into a little room off the kitchen. She wanted him to see her new day bed. He felt the springs as she had and praised the bed in her terms. He meant it when he said he wished he had one, and sat down on it. Mrs. Mathers left the room, and returned a moment later whispering that she believed in flushing the toilet before she made coffee. That was the quickest way to bring fresh water into the house.

170

Father Fabre, rising from the day bed, regretted that he wouldn't be able to pass this household hint on to Miss Burke.

Then, leaving the room, they met Mr. Pint, all salt and sweat, coming in from the back porch. He came among them as one from years at sea, scornful of soft living, suspicious of the womenfolk and young stay-at-home males.

The women followed Mr. Pint, and Father Fabre followed the women, into the dining room.

"You're a sight," said Velma.

"Your good blue shirt," said Mrs. Mathers. She went down the hall after Mr. Pint.

"We're going to eat in a minute," Velma said to Father Fabre. "You want to wash or anything?"

"No, thanks," he said. "I never wash."

He had tried to be funny, but Velma seemed ready to believe him.

Mrs. Mathers, looking upset, entered the dining room.

"Should I take off her plate?" Velma asked.

"Leave it on in case she does come," Mrs. Mathers said. "Father, you know Grace."

"No, I don't think so."

"Grace Halloran. She's in the Society."

"Of course." Of course he knew Grace, a maiden lady. He saw her almost daily, a shadow moving around the sanctuary, dusting the altar rail and filling vases with flowers—paid for by herself, the pastor said. Her brother was a big builder of highways. She wasn't the kind to use her means and position, however, to fraternize with the clergy. "Maybe she's just late," he said, rather hoping she wouldn't make it. The present company was difficult enough to assimilate.

Mr. Pint appeared among them again, now wearing a white shirt. Had he brought an extra? Or had Mrs. Mathers given him one which had belonged to her late husband? Father Fabre decided it would be unwise to ask.

They sat down to eat. It was like dining in a convent, with Velma in the role of the nun assigned to him, plying him with food. "Pickles?" He took one and passed the dish to Mr. Pint.

"He can't eat 'em," Velma said.

"That's too bad," said Father Fabre.

Mrs. Mathers, brooding, said, "I can't understand Grace, though heaven knows she can be difficult sometimes."

"If she'd only come," said Velma.

"Yes," said Father Fabre.

"Vel had to work last Sunday and didn't get a chance to meet her," said Mrs. Mathers.

"That's too bad," said Father Fabre.

"Grace was my best friend," Mrs. Mathers said. "In the Society, I mean."

Father Fabre frowned. *Was?*

"I was dying to meet her," said Velma, looking at Father Fabre.

"Very nice person," he said.

"I just can't understand it," declared Mrs. Mathers, without conviction. Then: "It's no surprise to me! You soon find out who your friends are!"

Father Fabre applied his fingers to the fried chicken. "Well," he said, "she doesn't know what she's missing." Grace's plate, however, seemed to reject the statement. "Did she know I was coming?"

"Oh, indeed, she did, Father! That's what makes me so blamed mad!"

Velma went to answer the telephone. "Yoo-hoo! It's for you-hoo!" she called.

"She means you," Mrs. Mathers said to Father Fabre, who wondered how she could have known.

He went to the bedroom, where Mrs. Mathers, never knowing when she'd be called for special duty, had her telephone. When he said "Hello" there was a click and then nothing. "Funny," he said, returning to the table. "Nobody there."

"Vel," Mrs. Mathers asked, "was *that* Grace?"

"She didn't say, Mildred. Wouldn't she say who she was if she was Grace?"

"It was Grace," said Mrs. Mathers quietly. She looked unwell.

There was a rattle of silverware. "Eat your dinner, Mildred," said Mr. Pint, and she did.

After dinner, they retired to the living room. Soon, with Mrs. Mathers and Mr. Pint yawning on the sofa, Velma said, "I met some Catholic priests that were married, once." She had taken the chair near Father Fabre's. They were using the same ash tray.

"Were they Greek or Russian?"

She seemed to think he was joking. "They were with their wives, two of them—I mean they were two couples—but they said the ones that weren't married could have dates with girls if they wanted to."

He nodded. "It's only been observed among us since the eleventh century—celibacy." Velma looked doubtful. "It may be overrated," he added, smiling.

"I never tried it," Velma said.

"Yes, well . . . in some parts of the world, even now, there are married Catholic priests."

"That's what these were," Velma said.

"Maybe they were *Old* Catholics," he said.

"No, they weren't, not at all."

He looked across the room at the couple on the sofa. Mr. Pint appeared to be asleep, but Mrs. Mathers was trying to fight it with a *Good Housekeeping*. "That's a sect," he said, getting back to Velma. "They go by that name. Old Catholics."

"I wouldn't say they were that," she said.

He was ready to drop it.

"I met them in Chicago," she said.

"I understand Old Catholics are strong there," he said. "Comparatively."

There was a lull during which Velma loaded her cigarette case and Father Fabre surveyed the room—the bookcase with no books in it, only plants and bric-a-brac, and the overstuffed furniture rising like bread beneath the slipcovers, which rivaled nature in the tropics for color and variety of growing things, and the upright piano with the mandolin and two photographs on top: one would be the late Mr. Mathers and somewhere in the other, a group picture of graduating nurses, would be the girl he had married, now stout, being now what she had always been becoming. Mrs. Mathers was openly napping now. The room was filled with breathing, hers and Mr. Pint's in unison, and the sun fell upon them all and upon the trembling ferns.

"Mildred says you can't have dates."

Father Fabre looked Velma right in the eye. "That's right." He'd drifted long enough. He'd left the conversation up to her from the beginning, and where had it got him? "I take it you're not a Catholic."

"Oh, no," she said, "but I see all your movies."

"I beg your pardon."

"I liked *The Miracle of the Bells* the best. But they're all swell."

He felt himself drifting again.

"I enjoyed reading *The Cardinal*," she said.

So had he. He wondered if a start could be made there.

Mrs. Mathers, whom he'd thought asleep, said, "Why don't you tell Father what you told me, Vel?"

"Mildred!" cried Velma.

Father Fabre blushed, thinking Velma must have remarked favorably on his appearance.

"About the church of your choice," said Mrs. Mathers.

"Oh, that. I told Mildred *The Miracle of the Bells* made me want to be a Catholic."

Mr. Pint came to and mumbled something.

Father Fabre decided to face up to him. "Do you like to go to the movies, Mr. Pint?"

"No, sir." Mr. Pint was not looking Father Fabre in the eye, but it was as though he didn't think it necessary—yet.

"Why, Dad," Mrs. Mathers said, "you took me last Sunday night."

"Not to those kind, I didn't. Whyn't you let me finish? By Dad, I ain't so old I can't remember what I did a week back."

"Who said anybody was old?" Velma asked.

"Stop showin' off," Mr. Pint said. "I heard who said it."

Mrs. Mathers clucked sadly, too wise to defend herself.

Mr. Pint blinked at her. "You made me go," he said.

Mrs. Mathers saw her chance. "Ho, ho," she laughed. "I'd just like to see anybody *make* you do anything!"

"You can say that again! Tell him about your office, Dad," Velma said, but Mr. Pint would not.

From the women, however, Father Fabre learned that Mr. Pint had asked "them"—his employers, presumably—to build him an office of glass so that he could sit in it, out of the dirt and noise, and keep an eye on the men who worked under him.

"Why shouldn't they do it," said Mrs. Mathers, "when he saves them all the money he does?"

Father Fabre, about to address Mr. Pint directly, rephrased his question. "He has men under him? I mean—many?"

"Five," said Mrs. Mathers. "Before he came, they had six. He gets more out of five men than they did out of six."

"Two he brought with him," Velma said. "They've been with Dad for years."

Father Fabre nodded. Mr. Pint, with his entourage, was like a big-time football coach, but what was Mr. Pint's work?

Velma, who had switched on the radio, cried, "Lee!"

Father Fabre watched the women closely. Evidently "Lee" was the announcer and not some entertainer to follow on the program. His sponsor, a used car dealer, whose name and address he gave, dispensed with commercial announcements on Sunday, he said, and presented music suited to the day. They sat quietly listening to *How Are Things in Glocca Morra?* Then to *The Rosary*, one of Mrs. Mathers' favorite pieces, she said. Then to *Cryin' in the Chapel*. Father Fabre wanted to go home.

Lee came on again with the business about no commercials and also threw in the correct time. (Mr. Pint pulled out his watch.) Lee warned motorists to be careful on the highways.

"Don't judge by this. You should hear him on weekdays," Velma said. "Does he ever kid the sponsors!"

"He's a good disc jockey or he wouldn't be on the air," Mrs. Mathers said tartly. "But he's no Arthur Godfrey." It sounded to Father Fabre as though she'd been over this ground with Velma before. "Do you ever get Arthur, Father?"

"Can't say that I do, Mrs. Mathers."

"He might give you some ideas for your sermons."

"My radio isn't working."

"I'll take Lee," Velma said. She rose and went down the hall to the bathroom.

Mrs. Mathers whispered, "Father, did I tell you she wanted to call in for them to play a song for you? *Our Lady of Fatima* or something. She wanted it to come over the air while you were here. A surprise."

"No," he said. "You didn't tell me about that."

"I told her not to do it. I said maybe you wouldn't want it."

"No, I wouldn't." He was grateful to Mrs. Mathers.

Showing a little interest, Mr. Pint inquired uneasily, "What do you think of this disc jockey business?" He got up and turned off the radio.

"I'm afraid I don't know much about it," Father Fabre said, surprised to find himself engaged in conversation with Mr. Pint.

"Sounds kind of fishy to me," said Mr. Pint, sitting down again. He had opened up some, not much, but some. "You know it's just playing phonograph records?"

"Yes," said Father Fabre, and then wondered if he'd said the right thing. Mr. Pint might have wanted to tell him about it. Fearing a lull, he plunged. "Certainly was good ice cream."

"Glad you liked it."

After the long winter, gentle spring, the sap running. . . . "That's a good idea of yours when you make ice cream—bringing an extra shirt, I mean."

There was a bad silence, the worst of the afternoon, crippling every tongue. Even Velma, back with them, was quiet. Mr. Pint was positively stony. Finally, as if seeing no other way, Mrs. Mathers explained:

"Mr. Pint lives here, Father."

"He does?"

"Yes, Father."

"I guess I didn't know."

"I guess I didn't tell you."

"No reason why you should've," he said quickly. "You do have quite a bit of room here." He seemed to be perspiring. "Certainly do get the sun." He never would have thought it.

Was there a chance that Mr. Pint, who acted so strangely, was not her lover? He took a good look at Mr. Pint. Was there a chance that he was? In either case, Mrs. Mathers had planned well. Father Fabre, taking out his handkerchief, blew his nose politely and dabbed at his cold, damp neck. He was in very good health and perspired freely. The fat flowery arms of the overstuffed chair held him fast while the hidden mouth devoured him. The trembling ferns frankly desired him. He just never would have thought it.

"You should see my little room at the Y," Velma said. "So dark." She was looking at Father Fabre, but he could think of nothing to say.

Mrs. Mathers sighed. "Vel, you *could* stay here, you know. She could, too." Mrs. Mathers appealed to Father Fabre. "The day bed is always ready."

"Oh, well," said Velma.

"So I had this extra bedroom," Mrs. Mathers said, as if coming to the end of a long explanation, "and I thought I might as well have the income from it—what's your opinion, Father?"

"Swell," he said. In the future he ought to listen to Miss Burke and stay away from John, with his rotten talk against her. A very sound person, Miss Burke, voices, visions and all. He ought to develop a retiring nature, too, stick close to the pastor, maybe try to get a job in his war plant. "I hate to rush off," he said, rising.

"Don't tell me it's time for devotions," said Mrs. Mathers.

They went down the street together. "You know, Father," said Mrs. Mathers, "I almost asked them to come along with us."

"You did?" Mrs. Mathers was hard to figure. He'd heard that hospital life made iconoclasts.

"What'd you think of Vel?"

"Who? Oh, fine." He didn't know what he thought of Vel. "What does she do?"

"She's with the telephone company, Father. She thinks she's in line for a supervisor's, but I don't know. The seniority system is the one big thing in her favor. Of course, it wouldn't come right away."

"I suppose not," Father Fabre said. "She seems quite young for that."

"Yes, and they're pretty careful about those jobs."

"What I understand." He was in line for a pastor's himself. They were pretty careful about those jobs too. "What does Mr. Pint do?"

"Didn't I tell you?"

"No," he said bleakly.

Mr. Pint was an engineer. "But he never touches a wrench. He's like an executive."

"Where?"

"At the hospital, Father."

"At City?"

"At Mercy, Father."

Oh, God, he thought, the nuns were going to be in on it too. They walked the next block in silence.

"Who plays the mandolin?" he asked.

"He does."

They walked another block in silence. "I don't want to get TV," she said plaintively. She brightened at the sight of a squirrel.

"Don't care for TV?"

"No, it's not that. I just don't know how long I'll keep my apartment."

Was Mrs. Mathers saying that she'd get out of town, or only that she'd move to another parish? If so, she was a little late. By feasting at their board, he had blessed the union, if any, in the eyes of the parish. What a deal! It was too late for him to condemn the enamored couple, one of whom was out of his jurisdiction anyway (in parting, he had shaken Mr. Pint's hand). It was a bad situation, bad in itself and bad because it involved him. Better, though, that they live in sin than marry in haste. That was something, however, that it would take theologians (contemplating the dangers of mixed marriage, the evil of divorce) to see. He knew what the parishioners would think of that.

And the pastor . . .

At the church, at the moment of parting, he said, "You're going to be early for devotions." That was all. To thank her, as he wanted to, for the good dinner would be, in a way, to thank her for compromising him with parish and pastor. It was quite enough that he say nothing to hurt her, and go.

"I've got some things to do around the side altars," Mrs. Mathers said.

He nodded, backing away.

"You suppose Grace'll be inside?" she called after him, just as if all were now well between her and her best friend in the Society.

He had his back to her and kept going, plowed on, nodding though, vigorously nodding like one of the famous yes-horses of Odense. For a moment he entertained the idea that Mrs. Mathers was a mental case, which would explain everything, but it wouldn't do. Mrs. Mathers remained a mystery to him.

In the rectory, he started up the front stairs for his room. Then he went back down, led by sounds to the converts' parlor. There he found a congregation of middle-aged women dressed mostly in navy blues and blacks, unmistakably Altar and Rosary, almost a full consistory, and swarming.

"Could I be of any service to you ladies?"

180

The swarming let up. "Miss Burke said we should wait in here," someone said.

He hadn't seen who had spoken. "For me?" he said, looking them over. He saw Grace sorrowing in their midst.

"No, Father," said someone else, also hidden from him. "We're here to see the pastor."

"Oh," he said.

"*He* went out on a sick call," said someone else.

"Oh," he said, and escaped.

One minute later he was settling down in the garage, on the bottom rung of a folding ladder, the best seat he could find. He picked up a wrench, got grease on his fingers, and remembered that Mr. Pint never touched a wrench. He wondered where he'd gone wrong, if there was anything he might have done, or might yet do. There was nothing. He attributed his trouble to his belief, probably mistaken, that the chancery had wanted a man at Trinity to compensate for the pastor. Father Fabre had tried to be that man, one who would be accessible to the people. The pastor strenuously avoided people. He was happy with the machines in his room, or on a picnic with himself, topped off perhaps with a visit to the zoo. The assistant was the one to see at Trinity. Naturally there were people who would try to capitalize on his inexperience. The pastor gave him a lot of rope. Some pastors wouldn't let their curates dine out with parishioners—with good reason, it appeared. The pastor was watchful, though, and would rein in the rope on the merest suspicion. Father Fabre was thinking of the young lady of charm and education who had come to him after Mass one Sunday with the idea of starting up a study club at Trinity. He'd told the pastor and the pastor had told him, "It's under study." You might think that would be the end of it. It had been, so far as the young lady was concerned, but that evening

181

at table Father Fabre was asked by the dormouse if he knew about young ladies.

"Know about them?"

"Ummm." The dormouse was feasting on a soda cracker.

"No," said Father Fabre, very wise.

"Well, Father, I had them all in a sodality some years ago." (Ordinarily untalkative to the point of being occult, the pastor spoke now as a man compelled, and Father Fabre attended his every word. The seminary professors had harped on the wisdom of pastors, as against the all-consuming ignorance of curates.) It seemed that the pastor, being so busy, didn't notice how the young ladies showed up for induction during the few years of the sodality's existence at Trinity, but from the day he did, there had been no more of that. (*What?* Father Fabre wondered but did not interrupt.) The pastor was not narrow-minded, he said, and he granted that a young woman might wear a bit of paint on her wedding day. But when sodalists, dedicated to the Blessed Virgin, the Mother of God, Mary Immaculate, presented themselves at the communion rail in low-necked evening gowns, wearing lipstick, stuff in their eyes, and with their hair up in the permanent wave, why then, Gentlemen—the pastor used that word, causing Father Fabre to blink and then to realize he was hearing a speech the pastor must have given at a clergy conference—there was something wrong somewhere and that was why he had suppressed the sodality in his parish.

By God, thought Father Fabre, nodding vigorously, the pastor had a point! Here was something to remember if he ever got a church of his own.

It must have touched the pastor to see his point so well taken by his young curate, for he smiled. "You might say the scales dropped from my eyes," he said.

But by then Father Fabre, gazing at the cracker flak on the

pastor's black bosom, had begun to wonder what all this had
to do with a study club.

"A study club's just another name for a sodality," the pastor
prompted. "See what I mean?"

Father Fabre did not, not unless the pastor meant that
young ladies were apt to belong to either and that, therefore,
his curate would do well to steer clear of both. Hear their sins,
visit them in sickness and prison, give them the Sacrament.
Beyond that, there wasn't much to be done for or about them.
In time they would get old and useful. The pastor, for his part,
had put them away in the cellar part of his mind to ripen like
cheese. But the good ladies of the Altar and Rosary were something else again. Nuns could not have kept the church cleaner,
and the good ladies, unlike nuns, didn't labor under the illu-
sion that they were somehow priests, only different, and so
weren't always trying to vault the communion rail to the altar.

"You want to be one of these 'youth priests,' Father?"

"I haven't thought much about it."

"Good."

But, as the pastor must have noticed, Father Fabre had
wanted to get some "activities" going at Trinity, believing that
his apostolate lay in the world, with the people, as the pastor's
obviously didn't. Well, he had failed. But he wasn't sorry.
Wasn't there enough to do at Trinity, just doing the regular
chores? For the poor, the sick and dying, yes, anything. But
non-essentials he'd drop, including dining out with parishioners, and major decisions he'd cheerfully hand over to the
pastor. (He still thought the man who rented owls to rid you
of pigeons might have something, for that was nature's way,
no cruel machines or powders. But he'd stop agitating for the
owls, for that was another problem for the pastor, to solve or,
probably, not to solve.) Of course the parish was indifferently
run, but wasn't it a mistake to keep trying to take up *all* the

slack? He'd had himself under observation, of late. It seemed to him his outlook was changing, not from a diminution of zeal, not from loss of vision, but from growing older and wiser. At least he hoped so. He was beginning to believe he wasn't the man to compensate for the pastor—not that he'd ask for a transfer. The bishop was a gentle administrator but always seemed to find a place in one of the salt mines for a young man seeking a change. Father Fabre's predecessor in the curate's job at Trinity had been anti-social, which some of the gadabout clergy said could be a grievous fault in a parish priest, but he hadn't asked for a change—it had come to him—and now he was back in the seminary, as a professor with little pocket money, it was true, but enjoying food and handball again. That afternoon, sitting in the garage, Father Fabre envied him.

The pastor handed a wicker basket to Father Fabre, and himself carried a thermos bottle. He showed no surprise at finding his curate waiting for him in the garage and asked no questions. Father Fabre, the moment he saw the basket and bottle, understood that the pastor was returning from a picnic, and that Miss Burke, telling the ladies he'd gone on a sick call, thought it part of her job to create a good impression whenever possible, part of being loyal, the prime requisite. Who but the pastor would have her for a housekeeper?

They walked to the back door at the pastor's pace.

"Some coffee in here for you," the pastor said, jiggling the thermos bottle.

"Thanks," said Father Fabre, but he'd not be having any of that.

"One of the bears died at Como," the pastor said. "One of the babies."

"That's too bad," said Father Fabre. He pushed in the door for the pastor, then stood aside. "Some women to see you in the converts' parlor," he said, as the pastor passed in front of him.

The pastor nodded. Women in the converts' parlor; he would see them.

"I don't know," Father Fabre said. "It may concern me—indirectly." Then, staring down at the kitchen linoleum, he began an account of his afternoon at Mrs. Mathers'. At the worst part—his chagrin on learning of the setup there—the pastor interrupted. He filled an unwashed cup from the sink with the fluid from the thermos bottle, gave it to Father Fabre to drink, and watched to see that he did. Father Fabre drank Miss Burke's foul coffee to the dregs and chewed up a few grounds. When he started up his account again, the pastor interrupted.

"That's enough," he said.

Father Fabre, for a moment, thought he was in for it. But when he looked into the pastor's eyes, there was nothing in them for him to fear, nor was there fear, nor even fear of fear, bravado. The pastor's eyes were blue, blank and blue.

Father Fabre followed the pastor at a little distance, out of the kitchen, down the hallway. "Will you need me?" he said.

With an almost imperceptible shake of his head, the pastor walked into the converts' parlor, leaving the door ajar as always when dealing with women.

Father Fabre stayed to listen, out of sight of those inside. He soon realized that it had been a mistake to omit all mention of Velma in his account, as he had, thinking her presence at Mrs. Mathers' incidental, her youth likely to sidetrack the pastor, to arouse memories of so-called study clubs and suppressed sodalists. Why, if the pastor was to hear the details, didn't they tell him that Grace had been invited to dinner? Then there would have been five of them. The pastor was sure to get the wrong impression. To hear the ladies tell it, Mr. Pint and Father Fabre were as bad as sailors on leave, kindred evil spirits double-dating a couple of dazzled working girls. The ladies weren't being fair to Father Fabre or, he felt, even to Mr. Pint. He wondered at the pastor's silence. When all was said and done, there was little solidarity among priests—a nest of tables scratching each other.

In the next room, it was the old, old story, right from Scripture, the multitude crying, "Father, this woman was taken in adultery. The law commandeth us to stone such a one. What sayest thou?" The old story with the difference that the pastor had nothing to say. Why didn't he say, She that is without sin among you, let her first cast a stone at her! But there was one close by who could and would speak, who knew what it was to have the mob against him, and who was not afraid. With chapter and verse he'd atomize 'em. *This day thou shouldst be pastor.* Yes, it did look that way, but he'd wait a bit, to give the pastor a chance to redeem himself. He imagined how it would be if he hit them with that text. They, hearing him, would go out one by one, even the pastor, from that day forward his disciple. And he alone would remain, and the woman. And he, lifting up himself, would say, Woman, where are they that accused thee? Hath no one condemned thee? Who would say, No one, master. Neither will I condemn thee. Go, and sin no more.

"Think he can handle it?"

Whirling, Father Fabre beheld his tempter. "Be gone, John," he said, and watched the janitor slink away.

Father Fabre, after that, endeavored to think well of the pastor, to discover the meaning in his silence. Was this forbearance? It seemed more like paralysis. The bomb was there to be used, but the pastor couldn't or wouldn't use it. He'd have to do something, though. The ladies, calmed at first by his silence, sounded restless. Soon they might regard his silence

186

not as response to a grave problem but as refusal to hold council with them.

"We don't feel it's any of our business to know *what* you intend to do, Father, but we would like some assurance that something will be done. It that asking too much?"

The pastor said nothing.

"We thought you'd know what to do, Father," said another. "What would be best for all concerned, Father. Gosh, I don't know what to think!"

The pastor cleared his throat, touched, possibly, by the last speaker's humility, but he said nothing.

"I wonder if we've made ourselves clear," said the one who had spoken before the last one. She wasn't speaking to the pastor but to the multitude. "Maybe that's what comes from trying to describe everything in the best possible light." (Father Fabre remembered the raw deal they'd given him.) "Not *all* of us, I'm afraid, believe that man's there against Mildred's will."

" 'S not so."

Father Fabre gasped. Oh, no! Not that! But yes, the pastor had spoken.

"Father, do you mean to say we're lying?"

"*No.*"

Father Fabre shook his head. In all arguments with the pastor there was a place like the Sargasso Sea, and the ladies had reached it. It was authority that counted then, as Father Fabre knew, who had always lacked it. The ladies hadn't taken a vow of obedience, though, and they might not take " 'S not so" for an answer. They might very well go to the chancery. At the prospect of that, of the fine slandering he'd get there, and realizing only then that he and the pastor were in the same boat, Father Fabre began to consider the position as defined by " 'S not so" and "No." The pastor was saying

(a) that the situation, as reported by the ladies, was not so, and (b) that the ladies were not lying. He seemed to be contradicting himself, as was frequently the case in disputations with his curate. This was no intramural spat, however. The pastor would have to make sense for a change, to come out on top. *Could* the dormouse be right? And the ladies wrong in what they thought? What if what they thought was just not so? *Honi soit qui mal y pense?*

One said, "I just can't understand Mildred," but Father Fabre thought he could, now. At no time had Mrs. Mathers sounded guilty, and that—her seeming innocence—was what had thrown everything out of kilter. When she said Mr. Pint lived with her, when she said she was thinking of giving up her apartment, she had sounded not guilty but regretful, regretful and flustered, as though she knew that her friends and even her clergy were about to desert her. Mrs. Mathers was a veteran nurse, the human body was her work bench, sex probably a matter of technical concern, as with elderly plumbers who distinguish between the male and female connections. It was quite possible that Mrs. Mathers had thought nothing of letting a room to a member of the opposite sex. She could not have known that what was only an economy measure for her would appear to others as something very different—and so, in fact, it had become for her, in time. Mrs. Mathers and Mr. Pint were best described as victims of their love for each other. It was true love, of that Father Fabre was now certain. He had only to recollect it. If it were the other kind, Mrs. Mathers never would have invited him over—and Grace—to meet Mr. Pint. Mr. Pint, non-Catholic and priest-shy, had never really believed that Mrs. Mathers' friends would understand, and when Grace defaulted, he had become sullen, ready to take on anybody, even a priest, which showed the quality of his regard for Mrs. Mathers, that he meant to marry her willy-nilly, in or out of the Church. There must be no delay. All Mrs. Mathers needed now, all she'd ever needed, was a little time—and help. If she could get Mr. Pint to take instructions, they could have a church wedding. Velma, already Catholic in spirit, could be bridesmaid. That was it. The ladies had done their worst—Father Fabre's part in the affair was criminally exaggerated—but the pastor, the angelic dormouse, had not failed to sniff out the benign object of Mrs. Mathers' grand plan. Or what would have been its object. The ladies could easily spoil everything.

One of the ladies got sarcastic. "Would it be too much to ask, then, just what you do mean?"

The pastor said nothing.

Then the one who earlier had succeeded in getting him to clear his throat said, "Father, it's not always easy for us to understand everything you say. Now, Father, I always get a lot out of your sermons—why, some I've heard on television aren't half as good—but I don't kid myself that I can understand *every* word you say. Still waters run deep, I guess, and I haven't got the education I should have. So, Father, would you please tell us what you mean, in words we can all understand?"

It would have surprised Father Fabre if, after all that, the pastor had said nothing.

"'S *not so*," he said.

Father Fabre had to leave then, for devotions.

In the sacristy, he slipped into his cassock, eased the zipper past the spot where it stuck, pawed the hangers for his surplice, found it on the floor. The altar boys had come, but he wasn't in the mood for them, for the deceptive small talk that he seemed to do so well, from ballplayers to St. John Bosco in one leap, using the Socratic method to get them to do their own thinking and then breaking off the conversation when he'd brought out the best in them. It wasn't necessary with the two on hand—twins who were going to be priests anyway, according to them at the age of ten. They had fired the censer too soon, and it would be petering out after the rosary, when it would be needed for benediction. He stood at the door of the sacristy and gazed out into the almost empty church. It was the nice weather that kept people away from devotions, it was said, and it was the bad weather that kept them away in the wintertime. He saw Mrs. Mathers kneeling alone in prayer. The pastor had done well for her, everything considered, but not well enough, Father Fabre feared. He feared a scandal. Great schisms from little squabbles grew . . .

And great affirmations! He'd expected the pastor to dismiss the ladies in time for devotions, but he hadn't expected them to come, not in such numbers, and he took it as a sign from heaven when they didn't kneel apart from Mrs. Mathers, the woman taken in adultery, or thereabouts, a sign that the pastor had triumphed, as truth must always triumph over error, sooner or later, always: that was heaven's promise to pastors. Life was a dark business for everyone in it, but the way for pastors was ever lit by flares of special grace. Father Fabre, knowing full well that he, in spirit, had been no better than the ladies, thanked God for the little patience he'd had, and asked forgiveness for thinking ill of the pastor, for coveting his authority. He who would have been proud to hurl the ready answer at Mrs. Mathers' persecutors, to stone them back, to lose the ninety-nine sheep and save not the one whose innocence he would have violated publicly then as he had in his heart, in his heart humbled himself with thoughts of his unworthiness, marveled at the great good lesson he'd learned that day from the pastor, that Solomon. But the pastor, he knew, was zealous in matters affecting the common weal, champion of decency in his demesne, and might have a word or two for his curate at table that evening, and for Mrs. Mathers there would certainly be a just poke or two from the blunt sword of his mercy.

Father Fabre, trailing the boys out of the sacristy, gazed upon the peaceful flock, and then beyond, in a dim, dell-like recess of the nave used for baptism, he saw the shepherd carrying a stick and then he heard him opening a few windows.